An Occasional Dream
❧ Mike Lester ❧

UGLYTOWN

❧ LOS ANGELES ❧

First Edition

Text copyright © 2002 by Mike Lester. All Rights Reserved.

UGLYTOWN AND THE UGLYTOWN COIN LOGO SERVICEMARK REG. U.S. PAT. OFF.

.

Library of Congress Cataloging-in-Publication Data
Lester, Mike, 1970—
An occasional dream / by Mike Lester.—1st ed.
p. cm.
ISBN 0-9663473-8-2
1. City and town life—Fiction.
2. Criminals—Fiction.
I. Title.
PS3612.E47 O23   2002
813'.6—dc21   2002008283
CIP

Find out more of the mystery: UglyTown.com/Dream

Printed in the United States of America

10 9 8 7 6 5 4 3 2 1

In memory of Carrie Cooper—

Who told me I could, and that I would, many years ago.

All beautiful women are murderers. You've probably heard it said before.

AN OCCASIONAL DREAM

I

∞ BOOTS AND BANGS ∞

From the *East Bay Register* (Sep. 4, pg. 27):

FALMOUTH HEIGHTS — Police discovered the body of a man believed to have been shot at point-blank range as he rested in his car early Thursday.

A transient found Joseph Steadman, 37, this morning with a gunshot wound to his head. Steadman appeared to have been reclining in the driver's seat of his car, which was pulled to the side of the road.

"He probably pulled over to rest," said Detective Jim Butterfield of the Falmouth Heights Police Department.

"I want you to go to a party tonight."

Russ leaned back in his chair, disappearing in darkness.

"I just came from one."

"Don't want you drinking. I want you working. A guy owes me something."

I moved into the circle of light and lit up, the tip of my cigarette a firefly.

"What's he got? Money? Drugs?"

Russ shook his head, doing an admirable job for someone whose head rested squarely on his shoulders. Tufts of hair slithered from his shirt collar like snakes after a heavy rain.

"He's got something that I want. An address book. He's seen things."

I nodded the affirmative, dragging deeply, feeling the hot sting of smoke in my throat. It felt good. Tasted good.

"Little red book. Motherfucker carries it around everywhere with him." Russ was getting agitated, gesturing as he spoke. Smoldering. Brooding.

"What's he into?" I sat down.

"Coke. Girls. Son-of-a-bitch owns half the snatch in town." Russ ran a hand along the top of his head, its baldness reflecting a tiny point of light. "He's got things in that book we need."

Clark sat behind me, near the door.

"What's he got in there? You want to look up all his ladies?"

Russ leaned forward, his face emerging from the black. "That's none of your fucking business! I just want that book! I don't want him to even know it's missing." His face softened, as much as he could manage.

"Listen, kid, I know that sometimes I can be an asshole." Russ's gaze drifted over my shoulder for a moment, then his eyes found me, fixed on me. "But right now I got more important things on my mind. I've got a lot of things going on right now. You're part of the action. There's nothing on you." He poked a stuffy index finger against his desk, emphasizing the words. "You're a fucking phantom."

I exhaled a pale plume through my nostrils.

Russ grunted, his mass shifting slightly. "Leo. Young bastard. About your age. Lives on a boat. He's got a little office somewhere on the damned thing." His brow creased, eyes squinting. "Clark, what's that damn boat called? *Testosterone ... Toaster-oven ...*"

"*Testament.*"

"*Testament.* What a little prick." Russ leveled on me. "You'll get your usual take when you bring me the book. I might even throw in something extra." He rubbed his forehead. "All this excitement's getting to me. Clark, get me a Scotch. What about you? How 'bout some soda? What about a Tab? Mr. Pibb?"

I just leaned back, smoking, being dragged in.

two

We headed to the marina, Clark and I. Went through downtown, the neon of delis and strip bars shining down, pink and blue cotton candy blur. I chewed an aspirin and closed my eyes. We didn't speak.

✻

Clark parked on a hill overlooking the water. Concrete steps led to the docks below. A long way down. He reached back over his shoulder, pulled out a small briefcase, popped the latches.

"Check that." He pushed the Beretta into my hands. Full clip. I popped it in. Clark raised a pair of binoculars and scanned the docks. I watched his jaw clench.

"Why isn't Vaughn here for this?"

"Did anybody say he would be? You need to get with it, get with the fucking program. Don't you dare fuck this up!"

He looked through the binoculars again, back through the windshield to the floating cityscape of boats below. Colors played across his face, moved like the shadows of clouds. They faded, changed yellow, orange, then red. Deep scarlet.

"Are you some kind of pussy? Can't do it alone?" He never took his eyes off the boats.

He was trying to make me angry. To confuse me. Make me do something stupid.

Tense bastard.

"There it is."

There it was. 60-foot. A burst of colored paper lanterns. She was beautiful. Docked ten slips away from the steps.

"Nobody out front, nobody guarding it. This'll be easier than we thought." Clark's lips stretched thin. Devil face. Only later did I realize he was grinning. "You could just walk right in."

I stashed the gun in my coat pocket. "We'll see about that."

Clark lowered the binoculars, turned to me. "You know, I don't give a rat's ass about you. I think you're an unreliable jerk-off. I just want you to know I've been watching you, and I'm gonna keep on watching you. You're up to something. I can't prove it yet, but I can smell it. I'll be watching you all the time, boy-o."

I popped another aspirin, chewed. "Always a pleasure." Opened the door and got out.

The night was cold. The city on the other side of the bay shined on.

✶

I walked down the steps, watching my breath fog up and drift away into the darkness, wondering why I was doing this.

Money.

Lack of it. Money held me down. Russ had cut me a break. I was silent, untraceable. If it wasn't for this, I'd be dead.

Leo Richards. When he was seven he'd stabbed a burglar to death. Killed him with a knife that looked almost as big as his own little self. They found him standing in his kitchen over this dead guy. He'd been praised for killing. Little hero saved his family.

It just got easier.

I walked along the pier, looking at all the yachts, and thought about Richards. I tried to think of the best way to get on the boat. A lot of cash to get yourself a yacht like this. A lot of cash. I walked along as calm and cool as I pleased, even started to whistle. I knew Clark was sweating like crazy, watching through the binoculars and clenching his damn jaw.

There was a guy standing on the pier now, hadn't seen him come down, didn't know where he came from. He staggered, glass in hand, then pulled his pants down and started peeing in the bay.

"Hey buddy." I walked up to the guy as he fumbled with his zipper.

He turned to me, smiling in drunken uncertainty. "Oh hiii . . ."

"Quit your pissing and let's get back in there. We could both use another drink."

The guy put his arm around my shoulder, resting his weight against me. Both of us smiling now. We stumbled back on the boat.

"There are just not enough … hours left in the day to do … anything …"

"I know, I know."

Clark must have been wetting his pants.

I set this guy in a folding chair on the deck. Nobody was out, a few empty tables and that was it. Paper lanterns lit us up. I straightened the guy's tie.

"You wait here, pal. I'm gonna get you a drink. Don't move now."

He gave me a little salute.

I pointed at him, as if he were a disobedient child. He grinned and nodded.

I stepped into a room larger than my apartment. Mirrors everywhere. Full bar to the right. Big TV. Glass table with lines on it, cut and waiting. Ready to go.

Nobody around.

I looked back out at my buddy. Still grinning and nodding.

✻

Went down below, down narrow stairs, toward the thumping beat of the party. Down where the action was. I walked through the hall, four doors on each side, all shut. The door at the end of the hall was open, yawning colored lights and the smell of flesh and booze. The party.

I stood by the door, out of sight. Took a peek in. Orgy. Limbs, backs, and butts all slammed together in a throbbing mass. I stood fully within the frame of the door now, staring at the sweaty mound below me, bathed in blue light, now red. Blue again. Couldn't tell where one body ended and the other began. Somewhere in there, I saw a woman's face. She was smiling, eyes closed.

Nobody to bother me; everybody going at it. I decided to check the doors back in the hall.

The first was a bathroom. Nothing. Quietly opened another. Bedroom. Empty. I went through all the drawers just in case. Nothing. Another bedroom. I had to duck out fast. A kid came out of the adjoining bathroom. Fifteen, no more than sixteen. He was crying and wadding toilet paper into small, marble-sized balls. He shoved one up his ass to stop the bleeding.

Tried the last door. An office. The desk was locked. Picked myself in. Only took a minute. More coke, porn, and a gun. Thumbed through the porn. Didn't take any. No sign of Leo's address book here. Not a damned thing.

Then I remembered what Russ had told me.

Leo had the book on him.

✺

Finesse. Sounded pretty, but it was necessary if you had to do something and do it successfully. If you wanted to keep your teeth in your head.

I'd learned the importance of finesse early on. From day one. Come a long way from peeling tape off broken windows and kicking in shutters with my childhood friends. A long way.

But not far enough. Adrenalin was starting to run through my veins. For me, things were getting tougher, not easier. I just wanted to go back to Vaughn's and have another drink.

✺

I was about to leave the office, scratching my head, wondering how I'd get the damned book, when I heard the voices. Out in the hall. They must have come down from the upper deck. Man and a woman. Couldn't make out everything, just words here and there, peppered with anger.

I let the door stay open, just a crack, just enough to peek through.

"... you come to me because you like it, you need it ..."

Saw him first, Leo, standing in silk boxers and a robe. Arms crossed. "It's your decision. Just don't come crying to me when it all dries up!"

She said something then, something about hope or maybe dope. Couldn't tell. Leo just shook his head, veins swelling on his forehead. He was wiry, lean. Hungry. A jackal. Very white teeth.

She came into view then, saw only the back of her. Tall, shapely. White skin and deep black hair cut short. Like a raven's wing. Miniskirt and black boots. Had her arms out, waving them a little as she spoke. Pleading.

Whatever she said, it just made Leo angrier. He pointed at her, eyes glaring. I heard everything this time.

"You are mine! I own you! You leave tonight—fine! But I'll come by, Missy ..." He trailed off, nodding, eyes like flickering flames.

She lowered her head, hid her face with her hands. I could tell by the way her shoulders convulsed that she was crying, sobbing silently. Bastard just stood there, staring. She wouldn't look up. He slid out of his robe, threw it to the floor, and walked off.

She kept crying, and after a while, let her hands drop, defeated. She looked up and turned around, and I saw her face for the first time. Through the sadness, the red eyes, and the smeared eye shadow, was the face of true beauty. Black bangs that lay evenly across the forehead, the darkest eyebrows, lips rose-petal soft. A young girl in the body of a woman.

She turned, started to leave. I backed away, thought she could hear me. As she went by the door, I thought that for a second her tear-stained eyes saw through the opening and into the blackness, and met mine. Her glance was sad and accusing.

I waited for the sound of her boots going up those steps. She was gone and I looked out. Nobody.

Grabbed Leo's robe and found the book.

✻

Went up top and took a beer from the bar. Popped the cap and sipped as I walked. Went out on deck, stood under the orange and red colored globes, and handed the bottle to my buddy. He gave me his little salute again.

This time, I returned it.

✻

Clark just held his hand out and didn't say a word. I gave him the book and the gun.

"Did anybody see you?"

"No."

✻

He dropped me off, telling me he'd be in touch. Russ would want to talk to me about everything. Clark sped away, and I climbed up the three flights, only wanting to sleep.

But I couldn't. I lay in bed, propped up on pillows, nursing a beer and watching the shadows on my ceiling. I thought of the girl and the way she had cried. Silently. Like there wasn't enough left in her.

✻

I finally drifted off. Had strange dreams of eyes and peacock feathers.

Restless sleep.

three

It got to be about noon, and I woke up. Poured a bowl of cereal and took it out onto the patio. Sat in the sun and ate it. Cereal always reminded me of being a kid. Strange, maybe, but it always had. Saturday mornings in front of the TV, spooning all that crap down. Good times. It was good to be a kid.

I sipped the milk from my bowl and thought about Leo's floating fuck-pad.

Some birds flew by, singing their song. I shut my eyes and turned my face to the sun. She was warm, and I soaked her right in. Felt good to find a quiet spot away from everything where a guy could sit in the sun and hear birds. Felt real good.

*

I was brushing my teeth when Vaughn called.

"Let's go get a pie."

I wiped the foam from my mouth. "You got it."

*

"So tell me about it." Vaughn grabbed a slice, mozzarella stretching back to his plate.

"Just more of Russ's bullshit. Nonsense work. He's involved with Richards."

"What did you have to do?"

"I took an address book. What for, I don't know. I thumbed through it, but I didn't see anything interesting. Just phone numbers." I ripped the crust off a slice, chewed it. "Did you know Richards likes little boys?"

Vaughn leaned forward.

"Young. Fourteen maybe."

Vaughn shook his head and reached under his hat, scratching his scalp.

I thought of Leo's eyes, black pools lined with dark fire.

The image of my father, his hair matted down with rain, came to me. His eyes were black, too.

I remembered the way he had stood, stayed after the others had left, and stared at my mother's bright marble headstone.

"I can almost see my reflection," he'd said, and later we sat in the kitchen. He had his butterfly collection at the table and was studying a monarch under a magnifying glass.

A wedge of fresh, amber-colored sunlight ran across his face, then it was gone.

✻

I said goodbye to Vaughn and went back home. Did a little reading. Waited for night.

four

The dark came up, chased the light away, and I rose with it. Streetlamps cast orange light through my window. Lazy sirens in the street below. Banshees.

I looked out the window, hands pressed against the cool glass. Looked at the buildings out there, near and far, all lit up. Glowing from the inside. A janitor was vacuuming in one, pushing that thing like mad. I leaned forward, forehead to the glass, eyes never leaving the towers. A light rain began to fall.

"What kind of sick shit is going on out there?"

From the *East Bay Register* (Sep. 15, pg. 22):

GILLESPIE — A married couple was gunned down during an attempted car-jacking last night, according to police.

Patrolmen found the bodies of Ronnie and Sandra Hayes in their car as it idled on Mason Boulevard. Each victim had suffered two gunshot wounds to the head.

A blown tire had apparently forced the couple to pull over to the side of the road. Police believe the gunman approached shortly after ...

five

"Kid, you did great."

Russ lit up, dragged in, rolling the cigar between his fingers. His office reeked of smoke. "But what's this bullshit Clark tells me? That you went on board with somebody?"

I straightened up. "Yeah, well, the guy was drunk off his ass."

"I'm not used to this from you. You're a ghost, remember?" Russ looked down, seemed to think for a moment, frowning. Nodded. "I trust your instincts, though. If you don't think this bastard could finger you, well, okay then. Here." He tossed an envelope on the desk.

I took it without opening it. Put it in my coat pocket. "Everything smooth?"

"Yeah. I don't need you tonight. Go on. Get lost. Spend your cash."

✻

Didn't catch a cab. Didn't bother. Fine misty drizzle falling, thought I'd walk. City lights a mirror image in the wet streets. Smell of asphalt and exhaust.

People hurried by, old men, busy in their way. A lady with a scarf on her head, umbrella resting on her shoulder like a rifle. I looked up, looked at all those glowing buildings, tops lost in halos of foggy light.

I felt mist on my face, felt it run down my cheek, and I thought of the girl.

I stopped, leaned against a phone booth. Ran my hands across my face, through my hair. Headache coming on. I chewed an aspirin.

An old fella came along. He had a trumpet tucked under one arm, and as he passed, he tipped his hat to me. Wicked comb-over going on under there.

I was still young. Had time. Plenty of time to get it together.

Time. I knew it was a lie. Had to do something, anything, soon.

six

We sat in the darkened living room, Vaughn and I. His girl sat on the floor, did lines, cut them with her ATM card. We didn't speak. Didn't need to.

We were dry. I tapped Vaughn on the shoulder. "Let's go smoke."

Climbed out the window, into the night. Sat on the fire escape and watched the traffic far below. We lit up.

"She's got a nice place here."

"It's a lot nicer when her roommates are gone." Vaughn unbuttoned his collar, loosened his tie. "I forget they're around sometimes. I keep peeing with the door open. It's embarrassing."

✻

We climbed down the ladder, down past all the other apartments, potted plants on window sills.

When we got to the street, Vaughn looked back up.

"Kelly's gonna be mad as hell."

I clapped him on the back. "No way, pal. More coke for her."

We went on.

✻

Small's was always crowded, always packed. We walked on in. Vaughn tipped his hat to the doorman with a quick, precise slice.

Took our seats at the bar. Gin and tonic. Clear.

I swiveled on my stool, turned and faced the crowd. There they were. Everybody. Faces I'd seen around, somewhere, probably in here before. Faces seen through a screen. Took a sip. Cool. Lime. Easing into the haze.

I must have been staring out at the crowd for a while. When I turned back to the bar, Vaughn was gone, off in the corner chatting up some blonde grinning gal. Good for him.

I ordered another drink.

Ruben came in and sat next to me. He smelled like he'd jogged all over creation. "Hey, Boyd." Coffee breath. I usually saw Ruben in the park doing his thing, shouting and bumming hot dogs off vendors. "What's new, my man?"

"Not much, Ruben. How's the poetry coming along?"

"There's three things one needs when attempting to write verse. First, a lady. Two, inspiration. Three, a meal. The square kind."

"Hungry?" My drink arrived.

Ruben scratched at his beard. "My soul hungers."

"Okay. I can dig it."

"I've only got inspiration." He grabbed some peanuts from the bowl, put them in his jacket pocket.

"Isn't that all you need?"

"Hey baby, weren't you listening? Inspiration is a beautiful thing, but compared to a woman, man, it pales." He reached in, peeled a peanut, tossed it in his mouth.

I was getting drunk. Halfway there, starting to feel it.

Ruben was excited, leaned forward and chewed his peanuts.

"See, a woman can take you up higher than you've ever been. She could hold you right up there and love you. And you could both look down on everybody and be thankful for what you have. One connection out of millions. Just think of the odds, man. Just think of the odds."

Another nut, peeled, and there it went. "If your karma's in order."

I nodded. Lit a cigarette. Ruben kept talking. I thought about my karma.

✳

Last call. We stumbled out, the three of us. Ruben untied his dog from a stop sign. Labrador. Black.

"How's my favorite girl? Did you miss me, Blondie?"

"Hey, why do you call her Blondie?" Vaughn searched his pockets for a light.

Ruben knelt down, scratched his dog, scratched her behind the ears, under the chin. "Didn't you ever see *The Good, The Bad and The Ugly*?"

"Yeah."

We parted, Ruben and Blondie disappearing into the darkness of the park. Vaughn and I walked back. Back to Kelly's pad.

Just wanted to lie down and really sleep.

seven

It turned out to be a sunny day, and I sat in a big leather chair wishing I could be out in it. Russ and Clark, I could see them through the window, talking, arguing. Clark had his hands out in a kind of helpless way and Russ just kept drilling on into him.

Didn't know what that was all about. Didn't want to.

✱

We were on our way. Clark was driving fast and Vaughn was complaining about it.

"Shut up." Clark didn't face him, just drove.

I closed my eyes and thought about green bills fluttering like autumn leaves.

✱

I guess this guy owed Russ and just wouldn't pay up. Or couldn't. Didn't matter.

I'd get my cut.

Clark pulled to the curb about sixty feet south of the house. We all climbed out and just strolled right up to the front door.

Clark rang the bell, turned to face us.

"This is my show." He made an even, sweeping gesture and turned back as the door opened.

Little old lady. Straight out of the cartoons. The cat, the bird in the cage. Those. She looked up at us, cautious or curious, couldn't tell which. Probably both.

Clark, he really charmed her, folded his hands in front of himself, smiled a big toothy smile. "Good evening, ma'am. We're here to see Eddie. You must be his mother I've heard so much about."

She smiled. A few teeth left in there, just kicking back. "Oh yes, yes. Come in, won't you boys?"

The door opened right on up for us. We walked in. The place smelled like a second-hand shop.

"Eddie's upstairs. Have a seat in the living room, and I'll go get him."

Family pictures all over the place. Old ones, new ones.

She moved to the foot of the stairs and yelled up. "Eddie! Son! There's some boys here to see you!"

Movement from above. Floorboards creaked. Someone heavy walked across a room. Somewhere, a door opened.

"What's that, Ma?"

"Come on down here!"

I kept looking at all the pictures on the wall. Portraits. Chubby kid with his parents against a background of blue. Big hair. Old portrait. I looked over to Vaughn, then to Clark. He was watching the old woman, staring at her back.

Eddie came down the stairs, sounded like two at a time.

"Who's here, Ma?"

"There's friends here to see you, Eddie."

Eddie turned.

His face went pale.

Clark rose.

"Hi, Eddie. Ready to go bowling?"

Poor bastard.

✻

His mother sent us on our way with waves and smiles. She even gave Vaughn a cookie. We all walked back down the stairs to the sidewalk, Clark holding Eddie by the arm.

"Just be cool, you fat fuck."

✻

Clark drove. Vaughn and I sat in the back with Eddie between us. Vaughn was eating his cookie. Eddie was shaking, scared. Kept on blubbering about money and time. Clark never told him to shut up, just kept peeking back in the rearview mirror. I caught his glance. He was enjoying all this.

We finally made it to the dump. Clark drove in with only parking lights on. Piles of garbage towered on each side.

Clark stopped, put the car in park, but left the engine running. He turned back to us, green dash silhouette. A goblin. I could make out his eyes. His teeth, white, like a vampire's.

"Well, time's up, my boy." Clark was grinning.

Eddie sat and cried.

✡

We stood around Eddie.

Clark had a bat, one of those small ones they sell at stadiums as souvenirs. It said *Dodgers* on it.

Eddie saw the bat. Lost it. More crying, more blubbering about money, more begging and pleading. I think he even wet his pants.

"Cut a guy some slack." That was all he could repeat after a while. He lisped. Slightly.

Clark charged him, hit him square in the gut with that bat, just really hit him. Eddie fell and rolled around, huffing and puffing, saying, "Oh my God," and "Help me," or whatever else he thought would work.

Clark moved to the legs. "Hold the bitch down!" Vaughn jumped on Eddie. I stood and stared. Clark was really blazing now. He looked up at me. "You son-of-a-bitch! Get your ass down here!"

I snapped out of it and jumped in. Clark brought the bat down on a kneecap. There was a loud snap and a pop. I could feel the impact run through Eddie's body. Eddie screamed, high and shrill, like a woman. Clark pounded on the other knee, kept working until it turned to something like jelly, and the whole leg bent backward. Bent the way no leg really should. Like a dog's hind leg.

I wanted to scream, too. Maybe I did. Couldn't hear it over Eddie's own shrieks.

Clark moved to the arms and did them the same way he did the legs. He grabbed one of Eddie's arms, held it, held it up like he was showing off a fish he'd just caught, and pounded on it until it blew out at the elbow. Blew out and back in a compound fracture. He stopped after a bit, rolled off of Eddie and tried to catch his breath.

Eddie flipped and flopped like a goldfish that had jumped its bowl. His mouth even opened and closed, puckered up, tried to get air.

Vaughn was dusting himself off. I managed to get to my feet, staring at Eddie. Clark brushed his bangs back, turned to us and said, "Work, work, work."

Then he laid into Eddie again.

✲

I looked out the back window as we drove off. I could see Eddie there, in the dark, still flopping and rolling around in the dust. He'd be dead there, soon, bathed in moonlight.

✲

Clark dropped us both at Vaughn's. Good thing. I couldn't be in that car much longer.

✲

We parted ways. I walked, headed for the trains. I thought of Vaughn. Neither of us had spoken after Clark sped off. We were dead. Dead on the inside.

Glanced in the windows I passed. Some guy was sleeping in a dark room, TV on, casting pale light. Kept walking. Some lady was making a salad. She was 35, maybe 40. Still pretty, but beginning to lose it. Dad and kid out on the couch.

I stopped and watched this family for a while. Stood and smoked, watching them. She brought the food in to Dad and the kid, and they all sat together, the kid with his comic books, Mom and Dad with their own stories. She said something and they all laughed. Couldn't tell what it was. Couldn't tell at all.

Misty night, moving in low. I threw the butt in the gutter and walked on. Started to drizzle again. Kept going. Vacant lot and muddy ground. A white rock was embedded in the mud, street-light bouncing off it, sparkling. It looked like a jewel sitting there, waiting to be plucked and hidden away. That's just the way of things though. Probably a billion black bugs under that rock. Something rare and precious, and the bugs just crawl all over it.

✫

Got off the train and climbed the stairs to street level. Full blown rain.

I had no umbrella, and I got soaked, but somehow that didn't seem to matter.

Walked under the marquee of the Rialto. Light bulbs sizzling, wet sidewalk sun flares. I stood under the marquee, out of the rain, and looked at all the movie posters framed under glass. The ticket girl watched me, pitied me maybe. I was a wet dog.

Stood and looked at this one poster, secret agent movie, underwater scenes with spear guns and sharks and everything. Then this guy's voice cuts right through to me. It's all I hear.

"Hey, Missy! Missy, wait baby! C'mon baby, I'll make it up to you!"

I turned fast, turned on my heels, and saw the back of the girl. She ducked into a cab. Fur coat and short black hair.

The cab took off.

That guy, he stood there in the rain, hair wet and flattened. He had flowers in his hand. Just let them drop.

✻

By the time I made it home, I was a sneezing wreck. Crawled into bed and lay there. Finally sleep came. Thank God.

✻

Dreamt of her.

She turned to me and smiled in a familiar way. I held her at arm's length. Then squeezed her tightly, felt her body push up against mine. I couldn't let go. Couldn't at all.

eight

I awoke to the sound of the birds.

Felt like I had a milky film covering my body. I needed a shower.

My hair was still damp. I'd stood in the rain.

I'd seen her.

✱

I got out of bed and stumbled into the bathroom. Parted the curtain and turned on the water. Got in and stood, the water running over the back of my neck and shoulders. I inhaled the steam, deep breaths, and soon I was standing in a cloud, a whiteout. I couldn't see anything. I held a hand up in front of me, but could only see vague outlines. The mist covered everything like a sheet falling over a bed.

Water whirlpooled at my feet, gurgling down the drain.

"I was sitting on my steps out front having a smoke and minding my own business, then I see there's a guy wearing a red hood standing over by the mail truck, and then I heard two loud bangs. The guy in the hood ran off into the park. Then I heard something like a dog howling or moaning or something, so I called the cops."

—Caller identified as "Leonard"
88.7 Morning Show, Sep. 26

nine

"Sometimes things have to be rough. Sometimes a situation comes to the point where action has to be taken. It's like that. Sometimes, as they say, shit happens. You gotta be ready for it."

Russ clipped the end of his cigar, lit it, rolled it between his fingers. He looked across the desk at me. Looked at me through smoke and flame. "I already talked to Vaughn about all this. I know you boys have taken care of things for me before. You've done that for me and you didn't ask any questions." He shifted, blew smoke. "That's the way I want to keep this."

I only nodded. I could feel Clark behind me.

"Clark has his reservations, but I feel you and Vaughn are ready for a more active role." Russ pushed my take across the desk and seemed to smile.

"Thanks."

I took my money.

✽

I sat and smoked by a chain-link fence. Looked across the docks at all the ships and wondered what they were carrying. Cars. TV sets. VCRs. All that crap from Japan.

Russ's car was still there. Clark had left about a half-hour ago.

Just kept smoking and watching the pelicans dive into the water. Didn't know how the hell they could see those fish under there.

Missy ...

Leo had called her Missy. At the time I hadn't thought that Missy might be her name. The guy at the movies had called her that, too. I knew it was her. Just a feeling. Maybe. I knew she'd seen me that night on the boat. Knew it. Felt her gaze.

Heard the sound of a car and turned to see Russ's Caddy pull out of the warehouse in a cloud of dust. Big bastard was leaving.

After he'd gone, I walked down.

*

Walked on down and felt the gravel shift and crunch under my feet.

It wasn't hard getting in there. I'd thought it would've been, should've been, but was pleasantly surprised. Picked myself right in, just like nothing.

Went all the way back to Russ's office. I could smell him in the air, half expected him to walk back in. His presence, cigars and Scotch, his ghost, it was in there. Soaked into everything.

I went through the desk, found the book, and copied down what I needed.

✣

Never really did anything like this before. I needed a drink. Downed a few and walked along the boulevard, the haze clouding reality, but painting a much prettier picture.

The people I passed, they didn't look me in the eye. Never did. No eye contact. Not a smile or a "Good evening." Nothing. I wondered if it was like this in my father's time. My grandfather's?

No connections. Anywhere.

✣

It was a big brownstone. A great old thing, ivy growing all across the front in a river of green veins.

I stood across the street. Lit up and leaned against a signpost. A few kids were in the street, playing some damn game and making all kinds of noise. I just stood and smoked.

Didn't know which window was hers. She was on the third floor, I knew that much. Lights were on up there. Nothing else, though. No movement.

✣

I'd stood out there for God-knows-how-long. The noisy kids

had long since gone in to their dinner, their homework, their nightly beatings, whatever.

It got to be dark. A chill came in, a fog. I had no coat and was about to take off.

Then there she was.

She walked down the steps, walked on down like royalty, graceful and effortless, little handbag swinging. And that was that. Off down the sidewalk. I could almost smell her perfume.

I couldn't move. Could only watch her go.

*

I started home.

Turned the corner and left her quiet street. Felt like I was on one of those moving sidewalks at the airport. Every stride felt doubled. I seemed to be passing a lot of people. It was kind of crowded, more people than usual. Faces, faces, and more damned faces. Like a collage.

I passed a diner and inhaled. Food smells. I tried to feel satisfied, as if I'd somehow had a full meal, but I knew that I hadn't. I began to wish I'd brought a coat along.

ten

There was a loud knock on my door.

I'd put a few away and all of a sudden the paranoia came on. Been sitting around all afternoon.

Then the knock.

I did a kind of drunken shuffle and crept to the door. Tried to be quiet. Probably failed. Looked through the peephole, expected to see some kid with a box full of candy bars and a shit-eating grin, but all I got was a faceful of Clark.

✳

Vaughn was already there when we came in. Thin plane of smoke, eye level, record on the turntable. Chet Baker. Russ was sitting in his big chair tossing M&M's into his mouth. Jaw just working those things.

"I just wanted to say that I'm really glad you boys could come by tonight. That's really good of you." Russ kept hunting for the green ones, fishing around in the glass bowl, finding one and picking it out like a sandpiper. "They're supposed to make you horny. Good Lord Jesus. I'd be dead by now."

I offered a cigarette to Vaughn. He shook his head. Shook it real quick. I was still drunk, every move I made seemed exaggerated, magnified. Tried to be real still, gripped the arms of my chair. I sat there, riding it out.

"I'm ready to offer you boys a bigger cut. Can you believe it?" Russ looked away then, just for a moment, but I caught it. I saw his glance, his eyes meeting Clark's, the look punctuating his sentence. Finality. Case closed. "I can trust you two. I know I can."

⁂

We went outside, Vaughn and I. Sat on a stack of tires and had our smokes. Kicked the gravel around a bit. Maybe we were both thinking about bigger cuts, or maybe we were thinking about all the great things we could get with bigger cuts. Or maybe, maybe we were thinking about Eddie and his blubbering and his mother and the bad way he died. Maybe we were thinking about those things.

Somewhere, we thought about Eddie and all the other Eddies we'd be meeting down the line.

Vaughn was the first to speak. "All that extra money is gonna save my ass."

"Yep."

"It's gonna help a lot."

"Yep. It'll help." Tapped my ash.

Clark came out, unfolded his overcoat. He snatched Vaughn's

cigarette, plucked it right from his mouth, lit his own with it, then stuck it back in between Vaughn's lips.

"Bullshit." Clark took one very long drag. "Bull-fucking-shit, I say."

I could only nod.

"My opinion of you still stands, Boyd." He turned to Vaughn. "You too, jackass. If you two ever hesitate like you did the other night I swear to God I will kill you myself. You are both fuck-ups. Always will be."

It was best to let him just say what he had to say. After a while he got tired and gave up. Tired, or maybe he couldn't figure out why we weren't reacting. Truth is, I just didn't care. So he left.

A little later, Vaughn asked, "You want to go to Small's?"

"Not tonight. Got some things I want to do."

✻

Couldn't really understand it myself, but there I was, back there, leaning against that signpost, looking up at her window. All those stories, those old stories I read as a kid, they must've been true. Pictures of sailors clutching rocks as their ship crashed all to hell. In the background there was always a beautiful woman. And by God, she'd be smiling at all this. So, there I was.

I knew I was looking at her window. I'd seen a silhouette up there, feminine, and there was really no question about it any-more. I waited. Waited for something. Didn't know what it was. Opportunity. Courage maybe. Felt like a kid, standing around, hoping to notice and be noticed.

*

The night kept going on, and I kept on with it, smoking and wasting my time. At one point, some guy in sandals walked by, glanced at me, and was gone. Half an hour later he came on back with a sack full of groceries and looked at me as he went by. I hadn't even moved. He'd probably worry about it all night, poor bastard.

Nothing was happening. I stood there cursing my pitiful self, and then there he was. Son-of-a-bitch just walked along, hands in pockets, proud of his wiry self. He was smoking and walking too fast, shirt too tight, just right on the edge. Leo Richards was paying a call. He breezed along and turned up Missy's steps. Trotted on up and walked into her building.

I stayed.

*

Leo took his own damned time. He was up there for a while. I sort of lost track of it all after the guy in the sandals, but I do know I waited at least another hour. Waited and watched some cats slink about. Wild cats, skinny and scared. Wouldn't let me get near them.

Then Leo came back out. Same as before, walking too fast, shirt too tight. He walked off, down the street, to the trains.

Then she came out, ran and stood on the sidewalk. She stood and watched him turn the corner, far off down the street. When he was gone, she went and sat on her steps. She folded her arms and held them close. She looked cold.

I watched her there, from across the street, and after a while I saw her rise. She turned to go back inside, ignoring the skinny, scared cats and kids. I lit a cigarette. Must've caught her eye because she turned and we made contact.

She was looking at me. Right at me.

I dragged in and couldn't move, couldn't really move at all, and here she came across the street, arms still folded across her chest.

She stepped up on the curb. "Hey." For one damned second I thought she recognized me. "I could really use one of those right now." She nodded at my cigarette.

I shook one out, handed it to her, watched her place it in her mouth, place it between her lips. I lit it for her. Flame cast her in orange. Smooth. She'd been crying again.

I guess that's where it all really started for me.

From the East Bay Register (Oct. 1, pg. 4)

...Police are urging motorists to exercise caution while parking their cars. According to Detective Jim Butterfield, "One constant in this case has been that all of the victims have been shot while they were in their cars." He added that people should minimize the time they spend getting from their cars to their houses. "This seems to be when the gunman strikes," he said ...

eleven

Couldn't tell what was going on. Everything was all mixed up, turned upside-down. Nothing stayed the same. Not even the weather.

One day it would be hot and muggy as all hell. People would walk around in their shorts and tank tops, walk around in a sluggish, slow-motion way. I'd see kids eating ice cream and old ladies using umbrellas to block out the sun. Anything to get rid of that sticky hot feeling. I'd see all this, and the next damned day it would be raining hard like nothing before, and those same old ladies would be out on the streets putting their umbrellas to some real use.

It was the strangest October I'd seen, then or since.

Unpredictable.

Like a person.

✻

We stood on the sidewalk and smoked.

She looked at me, hesitated.

Then:

"I've seen you before, haven't I?"

"Before?" I coughed, exhaling smoke.

"Yeah. I can't place it, but I know I have." Feline.

"I don't think so. Maybe on the street somewhere. You know you come across a few hundred people every day."

"Maybe ... I'm usually good with faces. I think I've got a photographic memory. I used to beat my brother at those memory games all the time when we were kids. Do you know the ones I mean?"

I didn't.

"You know. Of course you do. There are all these tiles on a board, face down, with pictures painted on them and you have to turn them over and match them. Of course you know ..."

"Can I buy you a drink?"

*

We didn't go to Small's. Went to some place called La Cave. Older folks in there. Dark, quiet. Lava rock walls. Torches. Large, dark paintings lined the walls.

So I sat there with this young thing and just watched and listened. I don't think I even said more than twenty words the entire evening. Didn't matter though. She kept it up, kept the momentum going. Told me all about her life, her family, brothers and parents, childhood, clothes, music. Everything. She told me how she was the only daughter out of four kids. She was also the youngest. She told me of growing up around boys. Of knowing only boys and their ways. She was excited about all of it.

I watched her. Watched her smoke. Felt like I was back, standing outside her building again, leaning against a sign and looking for shadows. Looking for something, not knowing what it was.

"Remember that TV show with the butler and the kids who come to live with their uncle? Remember that show? I must've seen every one of those things twice. Anyway, that's what it was like. Except I was the only girl." She set her elbows on the table and continued, "TV's the pits now."

I leaned back, out of the light. "They definitely make lousy TV shows now. Music, too." I paused for a moment, unsure of whether or not to ask, then said, "So what is it you do exactly?"

Her eyes widened just a bit, hardly noticeable at all. She leaned back. "I get by. You know? I make ends meet. What about you, huh? What do you do?"

I smiled. "I get by."

She nodded, looked into my eyes, her black pools seeming to dilate in the false, exotic, lava rock light. "I mean who cares, really? There's worse stuff out there." She looked down at the table, then back up to me. "Nothing should ruin the moment."

"We think alike."

She was happy I agreed, and leaned forward, face near the candle.

Drinks came.

Her eyes burned in blue-green fire.

We touched glasses.

❋

One drink became two, then three.

We were feeling it.

The veil slipped over my eyes, over my mind. Everything was relaxed; our meaningless conversation somehow mattered. Looked out across the room, across the lava rock walls, and wondered what in the hell I was doing here.

❋

Stepped out into the night. Saw her in that light. I felt the chill, noticed the breeze blowing her bangs.

"I hope I didn't bore you with all those stories. When I feel comfortable with a person, I forget to stop myself."

We were walking along the avenue, walking slowly, taking our time.

I put my hands in my pockets, felt coins in there. "Do you

know how long it's been since I've really enjoyed myself? Since I've enjoyed someone's company?" She smiled.

We passed under a street lamp, the two of us walking in pale light. Turned the corner and there we were on her street. No kids out, no scared cats, just tree-lined sidewalk, parked cars, and windows filled with TV light.

I saw the signpost I had leaned against. A feeling of déjà vu played across my thoughts and was gone.

*

I left her there, at the steps. Turned to leave.

Heard her. I turned back. Her silhouette framed in the door-way, framed by light.

*

Made it home and had another drink. Stared out at the night. Thought about innocence. Innocence wrapped in a streetwise package.

Thought about Leo.

twelve

"I'm about ready to kill somebody!"

Russ was on the go, up and cruising around the warehouse. "What the hell do I pay you people for! No good sons-of-bitches! Clark!" He threw a chair. I stepped aside and let it hit the wall.

Clark came running out of Russ's office.

There were some guys wandering around. Guys I didn't know.

Vaughn and I left. Went outside and smoked, leaned against some old crates.

"You know what's going on?"

"Nope. Can't be good whatever it is."

Inside, somebody's ass hit the floor.

Vaughn tapped ash. "I'm having a birthday party next couple of nights. You should come."

"What do you want for your birthday?"

"Hell man, I don't know. A record or something, I guess."

*

Ended up getting him a record.

We all went to his place.

It was nice and the night was clear. I always liked going to

Vaughn's. It was a house, a real house, not an apartment. Backyard and everything.

I stood out in the back and watched a drunk couple play on the trampoline. He jumped. She jumped. Up and down. Laughing. Listened to their sounds, their laughter, and it became part of my haze. Base and background of all my thought. It was all as clear as could be.

Drunken thoughts.

Thoughts of dark-haired girls with exotic eyes.

✻

The rains had passed. The night air was warm, like a blanket in the morning.

I needed to be alone. Didn't feel social at all. Walked down the road with no purpose, no aim, just wanted to be out in the sounds.

There were people out in front of Small's. A few sat around tables. Others stood, talking intimately. I wandered in among them, through them, to the bar. Some clown off in the corner was singing to himself.

Ordered a Guinness. I paid up and took it out front, sipping.

I heard her as soon as I felt the night.

"Boyd!"

The voice was feminine, perfect. Couldn't seem to find her.

"Hey dummy! Over here!"

Jenny sat at one of the tables near a light post. Some guy was with her, looking down his nose at me.

"What's a pretty girl like you doing in a place like this?"

She smiled. "Sit with us. Sit out here with us." She held up a cigarette, offered me one.

I sat. "How's the painting going?"

"Let's not talk about that." She exhaled a blue cloud. "What've you been up to? Last time I saw you was … one of Vaughn's parties."

"I just came from one. We didn't really get a chance to talk at the last one. Anyway, I've been doing pretty much nothing. Same old, same old."

"You look different. Older, I think."

"That's because he's in love!" Ruben was standing at our table, bottle in one hand, Blondie's leash in the other. "He's in love! The little vampire's sucking the life right out of him!"

"Don't be a bore. Sit down." She tapped ash.

Ruben raised his glass, smiled, and sat with us.

I eased back into it all and felt the warm, honey-dipped glow of drunkenness nibble at my neck. Warm. Good.

Jenny cocked an eyebrow. "What do you mean 'He's in love?'"

Ruben sipped, wiped the foam from his upper lip. "Can't you tell? Look at him."

I laughed. Didn't know why.

She turned her gaze skyward.

A feeling came over me, as if I'd been sitting alone in a dark room and someone had just switched on the lights. I felt it completely. We were in it, us three.

She looked back at me. "Who are you in love with, Boyd?"

"Who do I love? Never really thought about it before."

"Oh come on!"

✻

Time went on. Jenny found some others and left.

Ruben and I walked. Blondie stayed by our side, at our pace. Occasionally we'd stop to let her sniff a light post or a garbage can. Ruben never let the conversation drag, punctuating his words with hand gestures.

I listened to him. In an earlier day, he would have been called a seer or a wizard, probably would've been killed for it, too. Now they just called him a drunk, but that didn't change anything. Not in my eyes. I listened, and his words sank into me like water invading thirsty soil, everything profound in my stupor. Looked over at him. He was straight out of an old painting. One of those Dutch guys on the cigar boxes with the funky collars.

"Did you ever think about how time works?"

He was amused at my question. The red lights of a lounge

played across his forehead as we passed. "Nobody understands that shit. You with me?"

I nodded. Yeah, I was with him.

"Time. All I know is, it's time we had some good times." He pointed up to a storefront. Liquor store.

I went in and bought some beer.

❋

We walked along the avenue like we were Huck and Jim cruising with the current. Saw things, heard things we wouldn't remember in the morning.

In the haze, everything mattered.

After a while, I noticed that we'd moved on to quieter streets. More spaces between the buildings, even a few green spots here and there. I could see the wharf down the hill, in between buildings as we passed.

Soon we were in the park. Dark, moonlit solitude. I pulled out the last of the beers and handed one to Ruben. I cracked mine open, downed it in a couple of gulps, and threw my bottle in the bushes.

Ruben looked my way. "Boyd, man, please respect my home."

I didn't even apologize, just went and got the bottle. Couldn't be sure, but I thought I cut myself on the damned bushes.

"A man's pad is his castle, you know? Eh, Blondie?" Ruben

scratched her behind the ears, and she leaned into his touch.

I looked around and nature hit me. I felt the park, saw it, sanctuary surrounded by concrete and glass. "You've got a nice place here, Rube."

He laughed and said, "Come on. Up here."

We climbed a rock hill overlooking the pond. In the daytime, boys sailed toy boats in the water. We sat at the top of that hill, Blondie at our feet. In the pond below, the city, upside-down, a bright reflection.

"I've got something that will make our night complete." Ruben reached in his coat pocket and pulled out a joint. "Let's get Chinese-eyes."

Only took a couple of hits. Felt it crawl up my back and into my mind with the old warm tingle. Better than beer. Better than booze. It was good.

I lay back and looked up into the sky. Ruben kept talking. I fell asleep there, on those warm rocks, in the night, under real stars, the drug swimming in my head.

＊

So there we were, Tony Bennett and I, in a hot-air balloon. We were up above it all, sailing, gliding through a bright crimson sunset.

"Throw off some ballast, bayyybee!" Tony pointed to some

sandbags tied to the outer edge of the basket. I cut a couple of them loose and watched them fall, disappearing to a pinpoint. We climbed higher, smoothly, like smoke.

It was a good sized basket. Dinner table for two in there. Tony sat down, and I sat with him. We were both wearing white dinner jackets. White dinner jackets, white balloon. Tony's shirt had ruffles.

Tony lifted the lid off a serving plate and cut thick slices of prime rib.

"*Mangia*, baby. *Mangia!*" He stacked the meat on my plate, adding a dab of horseradish. "A little *au jus?*"

I nodded.

"Cheers. Atta boy!"

We both had Scotch on the rocks. I drank mine right down. "You were great in *The Oscar*."

"You're my kind of guy, Boyd! Everything's comped!"

I looked over the side, over the edge of the basket, at the green hills below. Some kind of garden party going on down there. Everybody else dressed in white, too. Men, kids, ladies with parasols.

"Never mind them. We don't belong down there, kid." Tony cut into his meat, took a bite. Without looking, he reached over his shoulder and pulled a chain.

Fire. Hissing red tongues. Flame lit us up and we climbed higher.

Tony leaned back, chewing, mouth full of food. He raised a fresh Scotch, downed it, swallowed. His eyes went blank for a moment. Then he held up Leo's little red book, his smile a million teeth long, and started in on "Rags to Riches."

✻

The morning sun hit me, crept in through my lids and I woke up. I was stretched out on the rocks. Blondie was up, sitting at my feet, looking out over the pond and the city. Blondie, she was an old soul.

✻

Days went by and I wandered through them, lost in the desert.

thirteen

Sealed it. Did something stupid and sealed it. That's all it took.

After I put the phone back in its cradle, I just sat in my chair, looking out the window at the fading day, feeling a schoolboy nervousness spread over my frame.

I remembered slices of conversation I'd had with Ruben the other night, sitting under the sky.

I remembered asking him what karma was and how could a guy tell if his was in order. I remembered worrying about my karma, if I had any.

Ruben had told me he used to walk through the park when he first arrived in the city. No money, nowhere to go, nothing to do. He told me that one hot summer day he'd been walking down by the pond, walking and trying not to think about any damned thing. The heat and sun made everybody sluggish.

He saw a small bird land at the water's edge. It dipped its beak in the water, ruffled its feathers, shook its head, tried to get cool. And Ruben, damned if he didn't throw a rock at that little thing. Threw a rock right at it and killed it there by the water. He said that as soon as the stone left his hand he knew he'd killed it. He said he didn't even understand why. He told me he saw the bird lying on the ground, the last traces of movement fading from it like the end of a movie, and he'd started crying.

He told me that he'd stood over this dead little bird that hadn't ever done him wrong and cried with his hands to his face, pure, like a child. He'd taken the bird and buried it in the plants near the pond, sat with it for a while, and had asked God to help him make up for what he did. He said he'd asked God to help him get his karma in order.

And I'll be damned if he didn't find Blondie the very next week. She'd been lost or abandoned, something, it wasn't clear. She was a mess. She'd been routing through some overturned garbage cans in an alley, and he must've made some kind of noise, or maybe she smelled him, because she looked up from her cans and just stared right at him. To hear him tell it, there was a moment of recognition between them. She just walked right over to Ruben and licked his hand. They've been together ever since.

Ruben told me that his meeting Blondie was proof that his karma was in order. His repentance had been accepted. He told me he felt that the bird was living on through Blondie, living with him because their souls were linked. He swears it wasn't the booze, so, yeah, it seemed his karma was in order.

I still didn't know what the hell to make of mine, but after the phone call, I started to think that maybe it was coming around.

✣

We went to the Rialto. They were showing *Breakfast at Tiffany's*. "You have to see it. You *have* to," she'd insisted.

So we went.

The movie was actually pretty good. Missy and I, we sat in the theater, in the dark, and every once in a while I'd look over at her and she'd be staring at the screen, hypnotized, oblivious to everything else around her.

On the screen they were having a party and a cat was walking around on some bookshelves. A man with an eye patch was talking.

I looked back over at her, watched her put some popcorn in her mouth, just a piece or two.

As the scene on the screen faded out, so did her face.

*

Went to Small's and sat at the bar. Glasses chilled just right.

"Cheers." Everything was dark. Calm.

I looked into her eyes, then at the mirror behind her. In them, the multitudes.

*

We walked out into the night. We were in the park on a tree-lined path. The moon was hidden, ringing dark clouds with silver. Bits of lonesome newspaper blew along the path.

Had that movie in my head, floating in my memory. I held her hand as we walked.

"Do you ever feel like that?" She looked up at me as we walked.

"Feel like what?"

"Like Holly. From the movie. She had the mean reds. Not just the blues. The mean reds. Do you ever feel like that?"

"Sure. Sure. I guess we all do sometimes. Don't we?"

"Yeah, I guess we do."

There was a low mist over the pond. We stopped and stood at the shore for a few minutes, watching reflections ripple across the water's surface.

Heard some footsteps. I looked down the path, down the way we had come. Darkness covered the path. I couldn't see a thing.

"Didn't your mother ever tell you the park is unsafe at night?"

I saw Blondie first. They drifted out of the blackness, moved through it, surfacing.

"You're likely to run into shady characters down here. Or worse … drunks …" He raised a bottle.

"Hey Ruben."

He smiled and stood with us by the water. Blondie at our feet.

We passed the bottle around and talked and drank well into the night.

✻

We left Ruben there in the park. I looked back once as he and Blondie fell back into dark. Watched them slide away.

The streets were quiet. Sometimes a car went by, quickly, on its way somewhere, and that was about it. We passed bars and coffee shops, small, furious groups of people in the night. She stopped and picked up a couple of pebbles from the sidewalk. Tossed them in the palm of her loosely closed fist as we walked, shook them like dice. Then she tossed them at a bottle lying in the alley we were passing, one pebble hitting the glass with a solitary clang. Buried treasure. A discarded bottle with a genie in it, waiting.

The clouds kept moving in. The air went cold and a few drops began to fall.

We started walking faster. Finally it all came down, really started pouring in, and we began running.

"Oh my God! We're doomed!" She didn't even look back. I heard happiness in her voice.

We were doomed. Doomed and laughing, running in the night.

*

Got to her place. Made it. We stopped at the steps, stopped for a moment, and let the rain hit us. I looked at her then, right into her eyes. Raindrops fell down her forehead, across her face. Didn't have to say anything. We were climbing those steps before I knew it.

*

She lit candles, and we sat in the dark orange dimness. Sat and listened to the rain outside, the wet, dark night. She'd made a pot of hot tea, poured it into cups.

"This reminds me of when I was a kid." Missy stretched out, lay back on the couch.

Then it was just the rain.

*

I wasn't sure how long I'd been out.

She had fallen asleep, a cigarette still lay between her fingers, ash way too long. Got up and stood over her. Looked down at her, watched her sleep, watched her chest rise and fall silently.

She stirred.

I moved to the end of the couch and unfolded the blanket she had draped over one side. I covered her and blew out the candles.

I was alone.

※

Stepped out in the hall, gently closed her door behind me. Put my coat on and looked up.

"Who's this?!" Leo stood at the end of the hall. He'd just come up the steps and was pointing at me. His brow was furrowed as if trying to reason, to see through a fog.

I didn't know what to say.

Footsteps below. Two more guys came up and stood next to Leo.

"She's mine."

His eyes flashed, lit up like they had that night on the boat, copper-colored snake eyes.

※

Leo drove. Missy leaned away from him, against her window.

I sat in the back, in the middle. Felt like Eddie. Felt like he must have that night. Thought that maybe this was what my karma was bringing me. Not Blondie. My karma was bringing me Leo.

Those guys next to me, they smelled like wet leather and booze.

Leo rolled his window down as we sped along. I could smell salt and exhaust. We were going to the Testament.

fourteen

The paper lanterns weren't lit this time, they just blew in the breeze. The rain had stopped. I was pushed forward by one of the guys, pushed forward into that big living room.

Leo had Missy by the arm. "We're gonna go have a little talk. Gary, look after this macaroon."

One of the guys nodded. Big fella with a little hat. Probably wasn't a little hat, but on him it looked tiny. He looked like a giant leprechaun. For one awful moment, I thought I might start laughing.

Leo took Missy off down the stairs and into the hall where I'd first seen her. She glanced back at me as she went down. I couldn't tell if she was more afraid for me or her. Couldn't tell at all.

Gary and the other one turned to me. "Why don't you just sit your ass down on the couch."

I sat.

They stood and stared, mustaches and porkchop sideburns. Gary was antsy on his feet, shifting his weight from right to left to right again. His hands were at his sides, clenched into fists. The other one had a very slight facial tic, the corners of his mouth twitching in an invisible grimace.

A foghorn blew somewhere, far off.

Then loud steps out on the deck. Heels. A couple of girls

came in. Young. Teenagers. Tight shorts and T-shirts under rain-coats. They came in and sat next to me on the couch.

"What are you two doing here?" Gary checked his watch.

"Nothin' going on out there."

One of them turned to me. "Do you date?"

"Okay girls, not now." Gary made sweeping gestures, shooing them out the door.

She turned back. Blew me a kiss.

Kiss of death.

✣

Leo came back up. He was wearing his robe and that was it.

"The girls were here earlier. I got rid of them."

"Sent them out? Good man." Leo nodded, thought, and faced me. He smiled a crooked smile. "I hear you're quite the charmer. Did everything but buy her flowers. Didn't get in her skirt yet though? That's okay. I'd have to charge you for that, and she's not cheap." He laughed. A madman's laugh.

I said nothing.

Leo looked at Gary and the other guy. "I thought I was being nice. I was giving him a break ..." He looked around, eyes widening, incredulous. "Wasn't I giving him a break? Gary? Rudy?"

"You were giving him a break."

"See." He shook his head at me. Pulled me in close. I could smell alcohol on his breath. "You need to learn a little respect buddy boy. You need to learn to respect another man's property. My property. She's mine. I own her. I literally, fucking *own* her! I bought her from her daddy. He sold her to me ..." Leo didn't let me go. He moved in closer still, put a hand on my chin, squeezed my jaw. "He sold her to me and I can do whatever I want with her. Ten minutes ago, I fucked her in the ass." He lowered his head slightly, almost seemed to tuck it down, and his gaze shifted. His eyes darted past me, as if he were looking over my shoulders, but they were vacant and heavy lidded, the eyes of a ghost or a sleepwalker. A zombie. "What do you know about anything?" He started to tremble, keeping his voice at a low, clenched hiss. "What the fuck to you know about anything? Shit!" He pointed his index finger against my head, like a gun.

I didn't feel it coming, couldn't have anticipated it, but right then I felt a surge of adrenalin within me, and I charged him. I charged him and landed in his gut. We fell to the floor. I had my hands around his neck, and I would have strangled him to death if Gary hadn't laid into me, fist in my face. Must've broken my nose. All I saw was blood.

"Thank you, Gary." Leo got up and tightened his robe while I rolled around holding my nose, warm streams of blood running down over my knuckles.

Rudy had been knocked down somehow. From my angle on the floor, I saw him getting up, dusting himself off.

They tied me to a chair. Picked me up off the floor and tied me to a chair. Tied me tight, arms folded across the back. I couldn't wipe the blood off my face so it just got into my mouth, ran down my chin. The metallic taste of blood.

"Son-of-a-gun. Where did you come from, pardner? I usually see this shit coming at me ... whatever. You're going to learn some respect, my friend. You're going to remember me." Leo was sweating. He was insane.

I couldn't breathe. Felt a burning in my stomach and all the air left me. Gary landed another punch in the same spot. I sucked in deep, trying for air, but couldn't seem to make it work. Then my head jerked around and all I saw was Leo, straining as he hit, over and over, my nose destroyed. Couldn't see out of one eye. Felt like my teeth were just falling out, hanging by the roots. Spat blood so I wouldn't choke, and I think a tooth came out with it. Couldn't tell though. Couldn't think.

Saw his grin before I blacked out.

✳

The sun was up. I woke up with a face full of gravel. Gravel in my nose, in my mouth, stuck to my cheek and forehead. Couldn't move. Just lay there, listening to the gulls.

After a while, don't know how long, I moved a bit. Just a little at a time. Just a little until it got easier. I pulled my legs into a fetal position, and about twenty minutes later, I managed to sit up. Felt my face. One eye puffed shut. Swollen. Too bright out.

I finally got to my feet and stood, bent over. Aching. Still couldn't seem to breathe right, and I think they must've kicked me in the balls a few times because I couldn't feel a thing down there. Yet somehow I could. The numbness itself was painful. Ached all over and prayed for death to carry me away on her gray, tattered wings. My face, my neck, my back, my arms, my balls. I ached all over.

Looked around. I was in the shipyard, further down. Much further down.

Pretty soon, I hobbled off, toward the city.

✻

It was a hell of a walk home. Made it though. Made it despite the stares. Asked a guy for a cigarette, and he just gasped.

✻

Didn't turn on any lights. I avoided mirrors. Went into the kitchen and ran some cool water. Cupped my hands and held them under the stream, the small pool of water, and splashed it across my ruined face.

I ran a finger through my mouth, prowling for missing teeth. Weren't any. All accounted for. Bloody water flowed down my neck, across my chest. Looked like my throat was slit.

The blinds were closed, but some sun managed to slide on in. I fell back on the couch and into sleep.

fifteen

Woke up at night. Bright sunlight was replaced by creeping streetlight. Didn't get up or want to move at all. My arm was asleep, tingling, and I couldn't feel the damned thing.

Heard a siren somewhere in the streets below.

sirens. always sirens . . .

Covered my face with my hands. Couldn't think about anything. Kept seeing Eddie in my mind's eye. I felt myself slipping inside, falling away into the haze. Black. Held a pillow over my face and muted the sounds.

sixteen

Nothing much happened for the next few days. I stayed inside, only going out at night for trips to the market or the liquor store or wherever. People stared. I didn't care. Just wanted to buy my things and get out of there. Just wanted to get back home.

✳

The sun was out, doing her thing, chasing away the cold air, the damp smells.

I needed some fresh air. Decided to take a walk. I put sunglasses over my swollen eyes and stepped out into the day.

I held my face up to the sun as I walked along. My legs and balls barely hurt anymore. I must've been stepping strangely though, because everybody seemed to give me a wide berth as I went by.

Didn't matter.

I'd get my cut of good times soon enough. Whatever the hell that meant.

✳

Ran into Ruben. He and Blondie were standing at a bus stop.

"What happened, man?" He stroked his beard.

"Came across the bad guys, Ruben." I stepped and fumbled with some matches, trying to light up. "They knocked me around a bit."

"Fuckin' A, they did."

"I'll make it."

Ruben scratched Blondie's ears.

I looked down into her thoughtful, brown eyes.

✢

Left them and kept walking.

Saw a kid a few blocks up. He pointed a toy gun at me and pretended to shoot. I pretended to be shot.

✢

The rest of the day passed by quietly. Heard nothing. Felt nothing.

More Tricks Than Treats This Halloween

By ANNE BRICE
CONTRIBUTING EDITOR

Falmouth Heights's reputation as a quiet city appears to be unraveling at the seams. Violent crime rates have risen 30 percent from this time last year, and there is apparently no end to the trend in sight.

Violent crime is not unusual in today's urban areas. What makes the Falmouth Heights statistic alarming is the uniqueness of some of the crimes. In Gillespie, a man dressed as a clown committed suicide at a child's birthday party. Two weeks later, a Buellton cab driver was critically injured when a passenger threw acid in his face. Apparently the driver, who had been on the job for thirty years, had argued with the passenger over payment.

One of the more bizarre recent cases that has caught the attention of the national media is an ongoing string of shootings which have occurred in the Mason Park common area that separates the suburbs of Gillespie and Falmouth Heights. Police have established links among the shootings and are now consider-ing this the work of a serial killer. As of yesterday, four people have been killed.

It was early last week, 3:00 A.M., hours away from daylight when another shooting occurred. Mark and Aaron Antibe, twin brothers, age twenty, had been driving all day, coming home from school upstate. They had just pulled up in front of their parents' house. What happened next is uncertain. Mark Antibe told police that he and his brother had just stepped out of the car and were getting ready to open the trunk when a man walked up to them and said something. Antibe said the man had "some kind of hood on." That's the last thing he remembers. Mark is the lucky one. His brother, Aaron, died from multiple bullet wounds this afternoon at St. Joseph's Medical Center.

Detective Jim Butterfield is convinced that the Antibe twins were the latest victims of the scarlet-hooded gunman. At two recent press conferences, he has even alluded to the possibility that the gunman may be videotaping his crimes as he commits them.

If this strange and violent trend continues through the fall, Falmouth

Heights residents may find themselves choosing to stay in at night. That would be a shame. We're expecting an unusually harsh winter in the city, and it would be a shame if Falmouth Heights residents have to miss their few remaining days of sunshine for the year. To quote Detective Butterfield, "All it takes is one bad apple …"

From the *East Bay Register*
(Oct. 7, Opinion Section, pg. 3)

seventeen

Russ ambled out of his office and into the muted, stale air of the warehouse. He leaned against a stack of boxes. "Good Lord Jesus! What in all hell happened to your face?"

"It's nothing. Just a fight."

"Somebody giving you trouble?"

"No."

"You know, if somebody's fucking with you, if you're in over your head, I can help out. We're like family here for God's sake! I mean it! You!" And then he looked past me, pointing at some guy unloading VCRs from a truck. "What's your name!?"

"Carl." The guy seemed nervous.

"We're just like family here, aren't we, Carl!?"

"Yes sir, Mr. Dawson!" He went back to his VCRs.

Russ looked back into my eyes. "See. Family. Work can be your family. The most important thing a man has in life."

I stood, uncertain. "Yeah. Yeah, I know. It's okay. Really."

"All right. But Jesus! If you've got problems …"

"I know. I know … thanks …"

Then it happened. The only moment of warmth I'd ever seen in his eyes. He squinted, smiled, put a hand on my shoulders. "Let's go for a ride. Let me get my keys."

He turned, shook his head, rummaged through his pockets, and cruised back into his office.

✢

The car seemed huge on the inside. It smelled like vinyl. I felt like I was sitting in the belly of a whale. I played with the window controls while Russ fiddled with his keys.

"I can never tell which one is the door key and which one is the ignition key. I swear to God, Boyd, if I ever meet the son-of-a-bitch that decided we need two keys, I'll kill him."

All I could hear was that damned commercial and Ricardo Montalban saying *rich Corinthian leather . . .*

✢

We drove down the sunlit boulevard.

It was a different world in the daytime. Jekyll and Hyde. All the mystery gone, dried up in sunshine and honking car horns. No place for a man to get lost. To disappear. No place to come alive.

The people crawling all over the streets were different, too. Sunlight had chased away the desperate. Chased them back into their apartments, their crack dens, their shadows. Back underground, like roaches. Replaced them with the elderly doing errands, and the dead making their money.

A cab cut into our lane, cut us off, and Russ hit the brakes. Something in the trunk shifted and rolled.

"Bastard!" Russ shook a fist at the cab. Then he grunted, looked apologetic. "Driving brings out the worst in me. It brings out the worst in everybody. Truly."

✻

I was careful. Set the ball on the tee slowly, like placing an egg on a bed of nails. As soon as my hand moved away, the ball disappeared in a rush of air and a blur.

"Shit … ahhh … sliced it. Son-of-a- … " Russ squinted, watched the ball arc, then drop into the bay. "Set me up again, Boyd."

I did. Again, the ball was gone as soon as I set it down.

"Aaaayyy … there she goes …"

There was a moment then, just a moment, in which I heard the gulls floating on the breeze.

Then:

"I know you really don't have a hard-on for dirty work. I know that." Russ stood, jostling his feet, lining up his shot. Getting ready to swing. "I suppose that's natural."

Another whoosh, and the ball went sailing.

I watched it go, squinted, hand to my forehead, blocking out the sun. The ball fell, bounced off a barge, and plunked into the water. "Looks like you hit it that time."

"Heh. I did at that." Russ looked away from the bay, turned

to me. "I could see it in your eyes. I could see it from the first day. After you boys took care of things for me last month, I could see it then."

I didn't meet his gaze. Couldn't. I put my hands in my pockets and watched the boats and the gulls. Looked out across the bay to the city, and I wanted to disappear in there. Wanted to get lost in that maze. I didn't speak.

Russ leaned against his club as if it were a cane. "I don't like it any more than you do. You gotta believe me. But what has to be done, will be done. You see?"

I finally turned to him, looked him in the eye. "I see enough. I just want to get by."

"Hell, that's all anybody wants. That's all I want, too. But I'll tell you right here and now, if anybody ever stands in the way of my ability to get by, if anybody ever tries to fuck me, I'll have to knock him down. You see what I'm saying?" He took his hat off, wiped his brow. "This fella you boys visited, he was a thorn in my heel. He was in my way. And you, you pulled the thorn from my heel. It'll only get easier. Trust me." He put his hat back on. "You'll see."

eighteen

Small's was on, alive and moving. Took my usual seat at the counter. Vaughn sat there with me. We both drank silently, not bothering to compete with the crowd. Knocked some back, warmed myself up; each drink disappearing as fast as Russ's golf balls had earlier.

"Took a ride with the old man today."

"Yeah?"

"Went golfing."

And that was that. Red Sea rolled back in and muted us, the lull and drone of voices, music, and clanking glasses falling on us. We drank on.

✢

Took it outside after a while. I'd had about five or six and was feeling like some damned monk hiding in the orchard, sipping the goods. Drunk and in charge of nothing in particular.

"So what happened to your face? Really?"

"Just in the wrong place at the wrong time, I guess. You know?"

Vaughn sipped, wiped foam. "Yeah."

Sounds came in. Car horns and chatter. The muted, fuzzed-out cry of the night. City sounds.

"The swelling's gone down a bit. I was a mess there for a while."

Vaughn nodded, lit a cigarette. "I expect you were. What you sow is what you reap, they say."

They said that all right. They sure as hell did.

✻

Kelly came along with about ten or twelve of her friends and they chatted up the place in a smoky, boozed-up whirlwind. A wave of feminine sounds and sights ran across my blurred *ojos*. Vibes and pheromones. Gals' night out.

I went in and ordered another Guinness.

Vaughn followed me in. When I turned around he was standing right behind me. I spilled a bit.

Vaughn leaned in. "It's quieter in here!"

"What?!"

"It's quieter in here I said!"

I nodded.

We sat.

✻

We walked, left them all behind. Vaughn brought his beer with him. The night was warm. We took it easy.

"I've been doing a lot of thinking lately." Vaughn looked over at me.

I saw it out of the corner of my eye. "What's up?"

"Nothing really. Just life, you know?"

"So what's to think about?"

"Just need to simplify things right now. Streamline."

"It's never gonna be like that, pardner. Not in a million lifetimes."

*

When I was younger and didn't know any better, when I was in high school, I read something by a guy named Kafka. Probably the only thing I remember finishing in school. In that story there's a guy, and he's stuck in a palace or some kind of place. He's got somewhere to go, and something to do, and time is biting him on the ass, so now's the time to move. Doors lead to hallways which lead to doors which lead to more damned hallways until it all just seems so fucking impossible. Well, Kafka, he puts this fella through a world of shit, and when this guy finally gets out of the place, there's still a whole city of troubles and obstacles waiting for him. Enough to make a guy just pack it in and call it a day.

That's how I felt when I saw Clark waiting for me on my doorstep.

nineteen

He picked me up and we went back through the city, back the way I had just come. I sat in his car, chewing aspirin and smoking. I thought about my useless train ride, my useless journey, and realized I wouldn't be sleeping anytime soon.

"Jesus, Boyd. Could you at least roll the window down?"

I rolled it down. The smoke escaped like the dead on resurrection day, ghosts sailing right out of the graveyard.

Didn't know where I was going. Didn't bother to ask.

But I did know.

Of course I did. I knew where I was going and why. Sat and rode on in silence.

✧

We were back at the docks, the warehouse up ahead, a black silhouette. Looked like a mansion.

Clark reached over and popped the glove box open. He pulled out a remote and pressed the button. One of the big metal doors at the side of the warehouse began to slide open. Reminded me of Ali Baba's fucking cave. We pulled in, Russ in our headlights, dead ahead. Some poor bastard, bloodied, was sitting next to him, a chain wrapped across his chest, arms behind his back.

We came in slowly, the sound of the engines trapped by four walls bounced back at me through the open window.

Russ turned and ambled toward the car. He held both hands out in front of him, as if quieting a throng of lepers at Lourdes.

"Shut her off! Shut her off!" Russ fanned his face. "Jesus! Good Lord almighty! Shut her off before we all choke to death!"

Clark killed the engine, and the night came back in. He opened his door, leaned out.

"Sorry."

"Next time you run in here this late, I'm gonna beat your ass back to Walla Walla!"

I watched Russ's shuffle, the struggle to step, his feet barely leaving the ground. I noticed the bloody pliers he gripped in his fist.

The man next to Russ had a greasy rag stuffed in his mouth, held in by duct tape wrapped around his head. I recognized the silent expressiveness of his eyes.

Clark reached back in the car, hit the remote again, and the loading door began closing in rusty protest. Impact, and all echoed to silence. Deafening silence.

Then:

"Move this shit out of the way. Good God . . ."

I got out of the car, stood and faced Russ. He saw me and started to smile. It faded, the corners of his mouth relaxed and fell. Silent regard, eyes lost in black shadow. Vague presence.

"Well, it's about fucking time." Quickly, to Clark: "What the fuck took you so long?"

"Had to wait at his place for about an hour."

Russ nodded, grunted, and looked from Clark to me. "Get over here, kid."

I went. Stood next to Russ, in front of the guy in the chair.

Russ looked down at the floor. His brow furrowed. "Clark and I have been trying to figure out how to make our machine run a bit smoother." He left my side then, started pacing. "You know, they say it's the small businesses that keep America going. The lifeblood of our country ... small business." He nodded to himself and kept pacing, didn't look up at all, just kept watching the floor. "They're right."

I looked over at the guy in the chair, looked into his eyes, and watched them grow wider and whiter as Russ moved behind him. Russ put his hands on the guy's shoulders and stood like he was standing at a podium. His stubby fingers gripped the guy's shoulders, gripped them hard, and I could see the pressure as he held him there. I could see flesh bunching up between the fingers. Even through the guy's shirt.

Poor bastard, sitting there, beat up, bloodied, but still

clinging to some kind of hope. I could see it in his eyes. A drop of sweat ran down his forehead, along his cheek. I watched it mingle with blood.

You're going to learn respect ...

I remembered my night on the boat. Remembered being tied. Remembered everything, my bruises still fresh.

Russ checked his watch. "We've got to keep our country running. Got to keep our business running. You've got to keep your boss happy, and me, I've got my boss to keep happy. That's just the way it is. For this business to run smoothly, I need you to run smoothly." He pointed right at me, cigar stub glaring. "I need you to do your fucking part! GOD! DAMN!"

Echoes all around. Cold.

He put the cigar back in his mouth. "Of course we all just want to get by! That's why we work. You just can't skate by on your ass! Rest of us sons-of-bitches out here busting our balls won't let you!" He started pacing again, hand rubbing his bald scalp.

Then he turned, pointed at the guy in the chair, fist and pliers shaking. "And this piece of shit! Tried to take bread off my table! Tried to take it away from my family!"

That guy in the chair, he just shut his eyes at all this. I think that whatever hope he held up to this point was quickly shuffling off to Buffalo.

I was vaguely aware of Clark standing behind me, near the car.

Russ shifted toward me, his mass lumbering. "Save us." His voice was flat, foreign. Like he'd been dubbed.

Save us.

Didn't know what he meant.

Russ held out his hand. He held out the pliers.

I looked from the pliers to Russ, to the guy in the chair. I did this maybe three or four times. I looked at each of them, and in those brief flashes my mind was engraved with their outlines. Shapes.

Eddie ...

The name played across my mind like some kind of tune, horrifying in its normalcy. My head seemed to throb. My sinuses cleared. My vision went blurry, then everything went bright, and for one moment, I thought I might pass out. I saw him, lying in the dark, huffing and puffing for air. Eddie's glazed eyes. Leo's. I tasted blood. My mind was clouded like I'd been blindfolded, the hangman's hood thrown over my head.

I snapped out of it, came to. When I looked down at the pliers again, the damned things had somehow ended up in my fist. Didn't even remember taking them.

I looked at the man in the chair, his head reared back, eyes rolled, widening like a crazed horse's.

You're going to remember me …

Clark, Russ, and I, shadows, moved in and tore the guy apart.

✻

The night moved on. With the blackness, the numbness crept back in and settled in my bones, settled way down in there. I was no different from Russ or Clark or Leo. No different. I was one of them. Me and a million before and after.

✻

I looked up through the sun-roof at the night and the blank, milky, staring moon.

✻

We dumped the body in the harbor. Pulled it from the trunk and lay it there in the night, not far from where I'd found myself the other day.

Clark grabbed the guy under the arms. I took the legs. We heaved him over the pier. It was quiet, then the splash. In my mind I could see him sinking, feet first, arms outstretched, his white shirt dissolving away into deep blue darkness.

✻

We didn't speak on the way back.

I walked to the stairs and started climbing them. Turned and looked back. The engine idled, and we stared at each other.

I understood.

Nothing had changed.

Clark was gone in cloudy, cold exhaust, tail lights a crimson jack-o'-lantern rushing away.

twenty

The laughter of millions couldn't drown out the silence in my head. It burned everything right out of me, and I got restless. I stood up and paced around my apartment for a while. Picked up a book and started reading. I never made it further than a page or two. I sat back on the couch and turned the TV on. Sat and watched the parade of late night idiocy, a tenth-circle freak show expanding, growing more grotesque by the minute as I was offered tarot readings, topless teens, and diet plans.

I flipped through the channels. Stopped on the news. Somewhere a plane had crashed, and people were putting yellow bags on the ground. Little ones. Here and there.

Pale old man Death. Made me even more impatient.

I got myself out the door, walked right on out of there, and into the living city.

✲

I walked, and my thoughts blended together into a lazy whirlpool. Memories on the slide.

And I'll be damned if all that restless, hollow energy didn't just drip right off me like mercury pooling up and rolling into the gutter. Maybe I could just keep on walking. Keep right on going. Walk until my shoes begin to come apart and the laces fray. Walk until the day they decide to crumble right off my feet.

With each step I became more aware of where I was and where I was going.

✻

But when I looked up to see I was passing by Missy's place, I couldn't remember how I got there. Didn't plan on it. Didn't even consider it.

I walked along the rows of parked cars and street lamps overhead. Looked for those cats. Didn't see them.

I stood there for a while, in the night, outside the building. Thought about putting one foot in front of the other and moving on, about saving myself the trouble. Instead, I put my feet on the steps, climbed to the door.

A gray, thin-haired woman was coming out the door, and I had to grab it before it could swing shut. She looked back at me as she walked down the steps, looked at me and my bruises.

I caught sight of my reflection in the door. Purple flesh. The swelling in my eye was down, but still there.

I've seen you before, haven't I?

I don't think so . . .

✻

I rang the bell and waited. Stood and waited in silence. Dim movement from the other side of the door. The urge to forget and leave rose up again. Didn't have time to think about it though. The door opened before I could move.

Her eyes looked through the darkness, into mine.

I remembered my bruises and said, "Feels worse than it looks."

"I was worried about you."

A dog barked somewhere. She leaned out the door and looked down the street. She looked me up and down, then took me by my arm. "Come on inside."

She didn't have to force me.

*

I sat in the same place I had the other night.

"Can I get you anything? A drink?"

"No." I smiled. "You know, I don't know what I'm doing here."

Missy put a finger to her mouth, shushing me, and disappeared into the kitchen. Cupboards were opened and shut, glasses clanked against each other. Then she came back, holding two glasses of wine.

"Chianti." She handed me a glass and sat on the couch opposite me. "They say it's supposed to be healthy, actually. Good for the blood or something."

I leaned forward, elbows on my knees. "Listen, I don't—"

"It's all right."

And that was it for a while.

Late night traffic sounds down below filled in the empty spaces. Held us.

Her place was sparse. She had a bean bag in one corner, the two couches and the small table in the center, a record player, and two Pan Am travel posters stuck in the wall with thumbtacks. Paris and Rome. Two white tennis shoes out on the fire escape.

I tried to lean back on the couch and relax. Thought about my face, and it started hurting. I sipped.

"I've been worried."

"I've been worried, too."

Then we laughed.

It wouldn't take millions after all.

✡

The poster on the wall, Rome, I looked into it, lost myself. Walked the streets at midnight. Drunk on wine. Walked along streets of betrayal, dark, shaded with antiquity. Hazy. Felt drugged.

Then her words came through, like God's own voice in the darkness. I snapped out of it. "Sorry."

"Let me get some more." She went back in the kitchen, and a moment later, came back with a fresh bottle. She held it out to me, some kind of glee flickering across her face.

I opened it. I could smell the wine's dry aroma. Took our glasses and tipped the bottle over them, filling them with dark liquid. Stained glass.

✻

Chinese food. Chinese food and all the little boxes that come with it.

"Here's some plates." She handed them to me. "I got these from my aunt. Look at the cool design on them. It's some kind of snake."

I looked. There was a snake circling the rim of each plate, a snake eating its own tail. I traced the pattern with my fingertips. Then I spooned the food out onto each plate.

The food was good; the wine's sharp, dark taste held me in its grip.

The street below was quiet, and we could hear the cars two blocks up.

I finished my wine and poured another.

✻

We lay in stillness and false moonlight, city dark.

Her skin warm and pale. Warmth in her arms. Deep embrace, deeper still, and it seemed eternal.

Eyes.

Mouth.

Then sleep, and a black raven's wing resting on my chest.

I dreamt of stars, the dark canopy of night.

✳

Didn't matter where I slept, the sun always found me. I rolled out of bed gently, without waking Missy, and went into the bathroom. Splashed cold water on my face, in my hair. Put my clothes on and let myself out.

✳

I stepped out into the cool morning sun. I didn't care about my fading bruises anymore; let them stare. Just a fact of life.

I walked off toward the trains. Took my time and read the writing on the wall. Names sprayed and crossed out all over the place. THE WATERMAN RIPZ!, someone had scrawled. There were carved jack-o'-lanterns in a few of the apartment windows I passed.

Halloween. Coming on in.

I walked out of there, down below to the platform, enjoying the morning and what I felt to be love.

II

☞ SOME VELVET MORNING ☜

"The bluebird of happiness must've shit on your shoulder."

His voice startled me, pulled me out of my thoughts. I looked up. Vaughn was leaning against my front door, cigarette perched in the corner of his mouth.

"What's going on?"

Vaughn stood up straight. "You tell me. You've got a Cheshire-sized grin on your face."

"I do?" I did.

He stepped forward, clapped me on the back. "Well all right, my man."

"Yeah, yeah. Let's go inside." I stepped past him and opened the door.

It was dark inside, cool, a contrast to the morning. Vaughn walked over to the chair by the window and sat down. Then he leaned forward, stubbed out his cigarette, and immediately shot another one out of the crumpled pack. He offered it to me.

"No thanks." I sat on the couch and leaned back. "So what's up?"

"Nothing much. Just thought I'd stop by and shoot the shit." He lit up and shook the match out. "So, who's the lucky lady?"

"Lucky? Hell. I'm the lucky one."

"Lay it out."

"Maybe I'll take one of those things after all."

He reached into his coat pocket, pulled out the pack, and tossed it on the table.

"Thanks."

Vaughn was tapping his foot, lost in some crazy beat only he could hear. After a while, he noticed me watching his personal mambo and stopped. He took a drag, tilted his head back, exhaled straight up. There was a quiet moment then, a moment in which we just sat and smoked in silence. He looked at me through a horizon of drifting smoke.

"I just don't like the way I'm feeling about all this. I've never done shit like this before and I don't know if I can handle it." His voice was steady, unwavering. But it was also urgent. "I think I'm getting myself in way over my head. I'm just in it for the money, you know? I never thought it would get like this." Vaughn tapped ash, and I saw that his hands were shaking. Just a little, but they were shaking. "I just don't like feeling out of control."

I struck a match, smelled the pungent sting of sulfur, felt like it was burning right through me. "I know what you mean."

Vaughn looked down at his feet, nagging worry crossing his face. "No, you don't. You can't."

I nodded slowly, finally bringing the match to my cigarette. "I can ..."

He relaxed a bit. "Yeah. Maybe you do."

"Vaughn, there's things about Russ, things he and Clark do

that I don't even know about. All I want to know is what I've got to do, and when do I get paid for it."

He seemed surprised at this. He started tapping his foot again.

I took a deep drag. "I do know what you mean. I've felt it too, you know. Don't know about the rest. I don't like it, that's for damn sure."

Vaughn nodded, smoke streaming out of his nostrils.

I leaned forward. "We're in the same boat. Just grab yourself by the bootstraps and hoist up. I've got your back."

He smiled. Shallow, ineffective, like a screen door with a hole in it.

We really didn't say too much more after that.

two

"Your momma spit shine them shoes?" The Mexican blinked.

We were picking up a package.

Clark stepped in front of Vaughn who was backing away. "No, but your fucking fat-assed sister does. After she sucks my dick. Quit playing bandito. Tell Luna we're here."

"Sure, sure . . ." The guy took a step back, turned, and walked down the service hall.

Clark faced us, not saying a word.

I stood, hands in pockets, and looked around the place. American flag. Mexican flag. Orange couch with a life-sized cardboard standee of a Budweiser bikini girl behind it. I looked into her vacant photo-eyes. Probably a million subliminal messages scrawled all over her airbrushed face, none of them having to do with beer.

"Hey fellas! Come on in the back! I want to show you something!" Luna stood at the end of the hall, arms out front, waving us on back. "Pleasure before business! That's my motto! So come on!"

Clark went straight back to him like a shark to a piece of tattered meat. Turned his head at the sound of Luna's voice and moved right on down the hall. "I haven't got all day. Let's settle this shit so I can get the hell out of here."

Luna smiled. "You just need to learn to relax." Teeth.

Vaughn and I followed Clark. He was about ten paces ahead of us, arms swinging at his sides as he walked. "I'll relax when I see the money."

"I've got something tasty here for you. So gooood ..." Luna's voice was thick and smooth, like a velvet painting in a crappy restaurant. "I got what you need, my man."

"The only thing I need is the money. Nothing else." Clark stopped in front of Luna. They stood, neither of them speaking.

"No?" Luna's teeth shined, little tombstones in the forest of his beard. "I told him not to worry. The neighborhoods around here are ripe. He just has to trust me ..."

Clark squeezed Luna's shoulder and turned to Vaughn and I, his smile fading. "You two wait out here."

Luna turned and shouted back into his office. "Adrian! *Dos cervesas!* Shit guys, I got you covered."

✻

Clark came out about fifteen minutes later, bulky black briefcase in hand. He was sniffling. Kept wiping at his nose. "Let's get out of here."

✻

The briefcase sat up front in the passenger seat, next to Clark.

We drove along the crowded streets. Everything was washed out. The buildings and people slid by in silent sunlight.

I leaned back, not thinking about anything, and let my head rest in the space between the window and the door. Looked at the back of Clark's head as he drove.

Vaughn was looking out his own window. He sat in almost the exact same position I was sitting in.

Bookends.

*

He came right out of the blue, right out of nowhere and slammed this guy. Funny part of it was, the old man wasn't even giving us any trouble, and had never given us trouble before. But there it was. Vaughn just unloaded on him.

The old man took the hit square on the nose, stumbled backward, one thin red viper slithering over his upper lip and down his chin. A moment of silence, and then he parked his ass on the floor with a solid, decisive thud.

I looked over to Vaughn. He still had his arm cocked back, ready to swing again. Veins were bulging on his neck, and I saw that he was biting his lower lip. He looked down at the man who held his hands up in a silent plea. Vaughn's hands were trembling, and I felt what he felt. Lived it.

I turned and looked down the frozen food aisle, through the window, to the sun-baked street.

Clark was out in the car, eyes closed. He was leaning back, one hand resting on the briefcase.

✱

Clark set the briefcase down on the desk.

Russ folded his hands in front of him and watched Clark fumble with the latches. Couldn't see the money inside, but the look on Russ's face was clear enough.

"All counted, everything fine?"

Clark sat on the corner of the desk. "All counted."

"Luna give you any problems?"

"Just the usual bullshit. Nothing serious."

Russ nodded and leaned back in his chair. "I hate working with them. They all stick together."

Clark disappeared behind Russ's chair, and I could hear the rapid twists and turns of the dial as he opened the safe.

Russ continued talking to no one in particular, "I wouldn't trust Luna if my life depended on it. Never turn your back on the son-of-a-bitch." Vaughn lit up over in the corner, and Russ's gaze shifted to him. "You boys are gonna have to learn how to deal with him. I want you both with Clark every time we make a pick-up. It's important."

Clark popped up from behind Russ like Dracula rising from the coffin or some fag magician on a TV special. He grabbed the briefcase, slid it off the desk, and as he did, I saw a flash of green. Lots of it. He started stacking the money in the safe. *Mr. Magnifico will now make the money disappear, ladies and gentlemen ...*

"You gotta be careful out there. Luna and his boys are rough customers. You have to be able to handle them. All kinds of assholes running around ..." Russ spun in his chair and watched Clark finish with the money. Before Clark could close the safe, Russ reached in and grabbed a stack of bills. "Come here." He peeled six crisp notes from the stack.

I felt like a bad kid in the principal's office. Russ handed three to me and three to Vaughn. I didn't look at it or count it. Just stuck it deep down in my pocket.

"You boys have a safe and sane Halloween." Russ smiled.

Mischief Night Jitters Keep City on Its Toes

By ANNE BRICE
CONTRIBUTING EDITOR

Concerning public safety, Falmouth Heights police are taking no chances this Halloween. Due to the recent string of shootings in the Falmouth Heights and Gillespie areas, police are doubling patrols over the weekend.

The police have told parents that their children will be safe as they trick or treat, and that, "We'll be right out there with them, making sure everything's okay," as Falmouth Heights police spokesman, Gary Ryder, said at this morning's press conference. Ryder's words do not mean, however, that parents should let their kids stay out all hours of the evening. Everyone should exercise the same strong degree of caution and street smarts they have been during the last few weeks. Halloween is supposed to be a fun holiday for kids, and it should stay that way.

The increased patrols come after a week of false alarms and few leads for detectives. There have been several bogus sightings of the so-called Scarlet Gunman over the last week. The investigation is still in its early phase, but with cooperation between law enforcement and citizen's groups, it could be wrapped up sometime soon. The police are asking the public to refrain from dressing as the shooter this Halloween.

Among the recent false alarms reported to police during the last week were two sightings of the gunman in Gillespie, near the Munson train station. Another false alarm was reported in downtown Falmouth Heights by Walter Orenson, who runs a shoe repair shop on Seventeenth Street. "I live upstairs," Orenson told reporters. "One night last week, Tuesday, I finished locking the shop, and when I got to my room, I heard funny noises coming from the back alley. When I looked out there, I saw this guy standing in between the Dumpsters. Couldn't see what he was doing. It was kinda hard to get a good look at him. It was dark, and when I took a second look, he was gone."

It seems that as the year is ending, Falmouth Heights is turning a corner and catching up with the rest of America's cities. Sadly, as it does, it leaves some of its charm behind …

From the *East Bay Register*
(Oct. 30, Opinion Section, pg. 3)

three

It was dark when Vaughn and I stepped outside.

"Kelly's having some people over tonight. You wanna come?"

I zipped up my jacket. "No, thanks anyway."

Vaughn shrugged. "Suit yourself. I'll see you around."

"Yeah. Take it easy."

Walked back home in the warm night, watching dead leaves stampede along the sidewalk, blown by the dry breeze.

✤

My window was open and the city lights beamed in. I shut the window and closed the blinds. All the shadows merged, blended together in the simple, uncomplicated dark.

✤

I woke up sometime later, and looked over at the clock. 3:05 A.M.

There was noise in the kitchen.

Shuffling. Quiet, shuffling footsteps.

Looked up into the darkness, tried to hear the sounds, to pinpoint them. Reached over to my nightstand, slid my hand past the alarm clock, and found the lamp. I didn't turn it on.

Moved my hand around the lamp's base, fingers trickling

through blackness like a spider crawling across a countertop. I felt the leather holster behind the lamp and pulled out the Beretta.

Swung my legs over and got out of bed like a blind man. I went to the door, leaned against it, listened.

Nothing.

I stood in the dark for a moment, shifting the gun from hand to hand, and tried to decide what to do. A voice from somewhere deep in my head piped up, *fuck it, if you kill someone in here it's self-defense and there's nothing anybody can do to you and you won't have to feel guilty about it at all nobody'll do shit to you nobody at all just like nobody did anything to Leo when he was a kid and stabbed that burglar, hell, they might even give you a medal for it . . .*

I cocked the gun and jumped out through the doorway into the living room.

He was coming toward me, moving slow, one foot dragging behind the other with an awkward, deformed step and slide rhythm. Behind him, the light over the stove was on. He moved in silhouette, a great, flabby shadow seeming to slither along the walls.

I remember reaching out to turn on the hall light. Did that before I even thought of shooting. I flipped the switch, and the light shone straight down on him, bounced off his bruised, bloody, hair-encrusted forehead, and melted down his face in a yin-yang pattern of light and shadow.

Eddie.

It was Eddie, and he was looking right at me, his black eyes tinged bloodshot red. His skin was pale, translucent almost. Blue-green veins entwined, like ivy creeping up a brick wall, traveled from his throat to his cheeks. He wore the same clothes I remembered him in, the knees and elbows shredded, flapping like a bead curtain as he stepped. I caught a peek of white bone at one elbow.

Eddie smiled at me, black teeth blazing among violet gums, and raised a tattered arm. He was holding something, a screwdriver or pliers, or maybe nothing at all. Maybe he was pointing at me.

I'd like to think I had enough sense to fire a shot. I didn't. I was lost in his dead eyes.

Then I realized he wasn't smiling at all. Eddie's lips stretched back even further into a tight grimace.

He was hissing at me.

I felt everything pour into me then, shock, guilt, the absurdity of it all.

I screamed as I woke up, my pillow soaked with sweat.

Happy Halloween indeed.

From the *East Bay Register* (Nov. 1, pg. 1):

Scarlet Gunman Claims 5th

four

I squeezed a dab of toothpaste onto my brush and stared at it. It slid off the top of the brush to the sides, snail-like. I looked up into the mirror, expecting to see black eyes staring back into mine.

✻

The sun was up, throwing her mid-morning rays all over the place. I felt her warmth on the back of my neck as I walked along the street.

What had Scrooge said to Marley's ghost? *You may be a bit of underdone potato* ... something like that. Couldn't remember exactly.

The streets were caked with the dried slime of smashed jack-o'-lanterns. Seeds lay splattered to the sides of the curb, dried in a sticky paste like a jumper's brains in the morning sun. Shredded toilet paper hung from most of the light poles I passed, catching the breeze and blowing in a lazy whiplash swirl. Felt like a tiny fish caught under the tentacles of a giant jellyfish. Foil candy wrappers sparkled like treasure or the ceilings of cheap motel rooms.

I was hungry.

Went up three blocks to Bennie's. I sat at the counter and

tried to block out the phony fifties ambience and every-body's loud voices. Had eggs, dry toast, and coffee. I watched the waitresses in their little soda fountain outfits hustle all over the place.

A kid at the end of the counter was shoveling onion rings into his mouth. I watched him, fascinated as he brought his hand up and sort of tossed the rings in there. Each time he did this, there was an instant where the onion rings were free, sailing in mid-air between fingers and mouth. He never missed a beat. Beautiful. Poetry.

I paid up and left.

✼

I was standing on a corner, waiting for the little red hand to turn into the green walking dude.

"Hey man. Can I buy you a doughnut?"

I looked up into Ruben's eyes. I smiled. "No thanks."

"Are you going to the tattoo parlor? . . . Do you want a hat? I know where there is one . . ." Blondie sat down at his feet, stared across the intersection, ears rigid, pointing straight up.

"I think I'm covered today, Ruben." I knelt and scratched behind Blondie's ears. Her eyes narrowed and she looked up at me. I gazed back into her dark eyes, trying not to think of Eddie.

"Hope you stayed in last night, Boyd." Ruben was looking down at us. "All the freaks were out on the streets."

✳

I walked back home, hands thrust deep in my pockets, head down, watching my steps. The freaks were out, yes they were. Couldn't shake them. Couldn't shake the dream, couldn't shake Eddie. No underdone potato here.

My steps grew hurried, blurred, and the sidewalk moved under me like a gray treadmill. I slipped on a page of soggy, wrinkled newspaper that was plastered to the ground and breaking apart in pulpy, cottage cheese clumps. I caught myself with an awkward little jig, and turned to see if anyone had noticed. All clear. I glanced down and noticed the headline: SCARLET GUNMAN CLAIMS 5TH.

I walked to the end of the block. Turned right instead of left. I didn't want to go home anymore. Couldn't stand the thought of being cooped up in there all day with thoughts of Eddie.

✳

I knocked. Small dried flakes of white paint fell to my feet like snowflakes. Faint noise from within, the sound of latches, and she opened the door.

"Hi …" Missy faded into a smile and leaned against the door.

"You want to go for a walk?"

✿

She changed clothes, and we went out. We walked along the streets, each step taking me further from my worries. We stopped at a cart, and I bought coffee.

"Did you do anything last night?" She emptied a packet of sugar into her cup and stirred.

"No. I just stayed in. A friend of mine was having a party, but I didn't feel like dealing with it, you know?"

"Yeah. Me too. I like to stay in on Halloween anyway. It's kind of fun to sit around and watch old horror movies all night. I even carved a pumpkin."

We started walking again, Missy sipping through the little plastic lid. Our pace slowed. We walked without rushing, without really even thinking about where we were going. It felt good. I liked it. I think she did, too.

After a while, we found ourselves on the outskirts of the park. The sun was almost directly overhead.

She tugged on my arm. "Let's go in the park."

We walked along the paths, along the edge of the lake. Daylight dissolved the dusky, pumpkin-scented aura of the night before. A flash of balloons went by and Missy pitched her cup in a garbage can.

Out on the lake, some kid in a boat cackled at something, sounding like an old woman. What it was, I'll never know.

We walked. My hand slipped into hers as the bit players in our lives passed by.

She was looking at me. One of her eyebrows raised.

We came around a bend, and I saw the rock. "Let's go over here." We climbed its smooth, warm face.

There were a few boats out on the lake, some joggers over on the other side, even a kid with a fishing pole.

Missy leaned forward, clasped her arms around her legs, and let her chin rest on her knees. "The sun feels good." She closed her eyes and turned her face upward, a smile on her lips.

I looked across the lake, over the tree line, to the huge clock on the federal building. It flashed date, time, and temperature, seven days a week, twenty-four hours a day, like a huge, mute cyclops towering over the rest of us and passing judgment. Then I closed my eyes and looked up with her. A bright red-and-yellow sno-cone swirl ran across my inner eye. I opened my eyes again and rubbed them.

Missy's head was down, pressed against her knees.

"Are you still tired?"

Her shoulders slumped forward. I realized she was crying.

"Hey, what's wrong?"

She didn't say anything, just kept her head buried against her knees. I put my arm around her shoulder, pulled her over to me. She didn't say anything for a while. Then she pulled away and brought her hands to her face. "I lied to you."

"What do you mean?"

"I lied to everybody ... Everything I told you is a lie ..." She sobbed quietly, as if it were her own secret. "Everything ..."

I stared at her, unable to say anything, like an idiot.

"I made it all up. My past, my family ... everything ..." She was crying for herself, not for some white lie she might've told or some make-believe childhood. She was crying for herself deep down.

A couple of joggers ran past the rock. One of them looked up at us, and I made eye contact with her. Her eyes seemed to say, *what did you do to her, what did you say to make her cry you insensitive asshole?*

I put my arm around her shoulder again and pulled her back over to me.

The kid out in the boat started cackling again.

She looked up into my eyes.

I held her there, on the rock, in the morning sun.

✣

We walked back the way we had come. She looped one of her arms through mine as we made our way back to her place.

When we arrived, she climbed her stairs, unlocked the gate and opened the door behind it. Then she turned back to me. "Thanks."

I didn't have time to reply. She disappeared into the hall before I could even wave.

The door fell back into place and the locks engaged.

five

I needed to put things in order. Needed to piece together my own personal jigsaw.

Small's was the place for that. Day or night.

I walked in, felt cool waves of air cover me, blanket me in the dimness. My eyes adjusted, and I sat at the bar. Ordered a beer and turned to face the wall of mirrors on the other side of the room. The three others in the place sat hunched over their drinks, looking like piles of rock in an alien landscape.

Somebody was playing the piano over in the corner. Light shone down on a mop of wavy brown hair. Couldn't make out the face.

I grabbed my beer and leaned back against the bar. One drink became three, then four, and on to five. Around drink four, my hands began to tremble, not much, but there, a low tremor. A ripple in my karma, as Ruben would have said.

That guy kept on banging the keys, tickled the ivory as if he were spinning a web, and the notes hit me, came to me from thin air. I heard every note, felt every note as they seemed to physically float past me. Seemed I could almost reach out and touch them. I followed them back to their source, back to the skinny man with all the wavy brown hair. I watched his hands move, each finger seeming to prowl over the keys, hopping unconcerned over the black ones, stopping, then off again. The music was full of color, dark and lush, arabesque.

I drank on, and my thoughts moved from one to the other, from Missy to money to time. I wished for a way to be able to help her, to be able to solve all of her problems. And mine. One smooth stroke.

The music stopped.

I looked up, shaken from my stupor.

Mophead stood up and pushed the bench out from under him. He closed the little lid that covers the keys and took his drink from the top of the piano. He threw a scarf over his shoulders, and I watched it settle across the back of his neck like a low mist. He wore dark aviator sunglasses. "Get me a fresh one, Rocky." A cigarette bobbed on his lips as he spoke.

Glasses clanked, and ice poured behind me. Rocky grumbled something.

Mophead turned and looked at me. "You play?"

"Huh?"

"Piano. Do you play?" He wiggled his fingers as he said this.

"No."

He nodded to himself, not caring how I answered one way or the other.

Rocky thumped a Scotch and soda on the bar. As soon as it was down, Mophead's hands were all over it. He took a deep gulp and tilted his head back, momentarily frozen. The lenses of his aviators caught the overhead light, and in his stillness, the bastard looked exactly like Neil Diamond. He pursed his lips and quietly hissed in exhalation. Then he stuck out a hand. "Name's Marcus. Pianist."

I shook his hand. "Boyd. Early riser."

"Pleasure." Marcus turned to the bar and tugged at the back of Rocky's shirt. "How long ago did you call that cab?"

Rocky was drying glasses with a rag and didn't turn around. "They said fifteen minutes, and that was five minutes ago, so's you still have ten. Why don'tcha relax, enjoy your drink, and get the hell off my ass."

Marcus turned back, leaned, resting both elbows on the bar. Same position I was in. He looked across the room to the now silent piano. "God, I can't wait to get out of here. I'm off to Paris. I've got a friend who says he can get me a job there. What the hell, you know? You gotta seize the moment, as they say."

I didn't say anything. Didn't want to, didn't need to. Didn't need the hassle.

The silence was cut by the sound of wailing brakes from outside. I looked over Marcus's shoulder to the bright glare of the glass doors and the street beyond them. Through the bright smears of a year's worth of handprints, I saw a yellow taxi slide to a stop, one of the front tires riding up on the curb.

"Your ride's here." Rocky bent at the knees and hoisted two black suitcases out from behind the bar. "See? Ten fuckin' minutes."

Marcus was off his stool and all over the bags like he was with the drink. He snatched them, plucked them up by the handles, and gave me a friendly nod of farewell. As he passed, he set one of the bags down and grabbed his Scotch. "Here's to us early risers!" Downed it and out he went. Neil had left the building.

Rocky grunted again, and I turned to finish my beer. Day crowds. Definitely funkier than night crowds.

I ordered another and tried not to think about the way my hands were shaking.

*

I left Small's. Headed for home. Having a buzz in the morning always felt wrong somehow, but I'd be lying if I said I didn't enjoy it.

Stepped off the curb between two parked cars and cut across the street. I saw movement out of the corner of my eye. Somebody else jaywalking. I looked, but saw no one.

Made it across. Headed to the trains.

six

I couldn't sleep. Spent most of the night lying on my back and staring up at the ceiling, not thinking about anything at all. I looked at the pocked, cottage cheese landscape up there and drifted, pictured myself shrunk down, tiny and walking around. It would be like walking on the moon, I thought. I could see myself standing on the edge of one of those ceiling craters with a golf club clutched in my tiny fist, and boy, I'd connect and that ball would sail way off, dreamy and slow in the weightlessness . . .

. . . into the haze, man, and when it swallows you, you never come back . . . never ever, Boyd baybeeee . . .

My eyes were getting dry, and I rubbed them. They teared up. I thought of Missy and what she'd said in the park. I thought about her eyes the first time I'd seen them. The haze was coming on, and I was caught, lost in memory.

✻

Midnight came and went. It was still dark. A blanket of quiet had fallen outside, the city sounds muted, almost gone.

I got out of bed and stood, stretching. I yawned, raising my arms over my head. Felt every muscle in my body relax. With that stretch, I found new energy. I was fully awake, despite the insomnia.

Went out into the kitchen and poured myself a glass of water. I stood in the dark, leaned against the counter and looked out the window at the buildings beyond. They stood, giants obscured by mist and fog, huge candles with their flames snuffed out. Lights winked in a few windows, just enough to highlight the buildings, making them shine. I looked out across the dark Emerald City. The place I lived in. The streets of imagination. Silence. No cabs scuttled along the wet pavement. Steam rose from manholes, and lights changed silently from green to yellow to red, reflections burning bright. Clouds moved in low, and a light mist was in the air.

There was movement down below. Someone had run along the sidewalk beneath my window, a dark shape wrapped in an overcoat. I saw it move between awnings from one building to the next.

It was Missy.

I put on a pair of pants and a jacket and went out into the night.

*

I stood under the glow of a street lamp for a while and looked for her. There was nobody out. I was alone. I checked the alleys between my building and the others. I went to each corner and gazed far off down the deserted streets.

Nothing.

The clouds had come down and everybody had disappeared into them.

In the distance, I saw flashes of lightning. I started walking, counting the seconds between the flash and the shambling thunderclap which always strayed behind. I'd seen this done in a movie somewhere, and had considered it a valid practice ever since.

The park was across the street and, at this end, was surrounded by a high brick wall, slightly elevated. Moss covered the brick, hung from the wrought iron at the top.

I walked parallel to the wall, watching the empty streets and the trees beyond them. Trunks disappeared and reappeared in the orange glow of the lamps. The grit between my shoes and the sidewalk was the only sound. My footsteps seemed to echo among the buildings. Felt like a little boy lost in a big, bad forest.

Movement. In the distance. The little shadow of a man stepped out from around a corner five or six blocks up. He stood next to a stoplight, and seemed to turn toward me. The "Don't Walk" sign flashed bright red above his head, like an aura. He didn't move. I felt eyes look right into me. He was still too far away to even see his face, but I knew. I felt it.

My eyes were going dry again. A warm tingle crawled up my spine. I kept walking and rubbed my eyes. They teared, and as I walked, I looked through blurred eyes to the shape on the corner. It wavered in the blinking red light. I couldn't see anything. Then he was gone.

I heard a sound. It stood out, the stark silence broken for a moment, then it was gone. Just like the man. Gone. It came again, further off this time, somewhere down the street.

click

Like the clasps on a flagpole gently tapping in the breeze after all the kids have left for the day, or the tap-tap-tap of the sprinklers in the park at night.

It came again. A light clicking. Pliers. Yes, it was pliers. Somebody had a pair of pliers, and they were tapping them together out there.

My eyes and my steps were still blurred, and I don't remember what I saw or thought or did. When I could think again, I was standing on the docks. Waves rippled along the jetty and the clouds hung low, moving across the surface of the water. Lightning flashed. I began my countdown again.

I turned and faced the warehouse, gravel crunching and shifting under my feet as I walked. Made it to the fence and put my hands up on it, fingers grasping like talons.

The warehouse was dark. No one was ever here at this hour. I walked along the fence, dragged my hand across the links, and thought about the money and what I could do with it.

A heavy chain was coiled around the latch like a python around a tree trunk. I climbed the fence. Barbed wire caught me at the top, and I felt the sting as my palms tore, but I grabbed on and pulled myself over.

I landed, my hands pushed forward into the gravel. Stood and wiped them together.

Another flash. In that instant, I looked up to the warehouse, to the dark façade, like a black cathedral against the clouds. Old wives' tale or not, I kept counting.

Felt something in my pocket, and I reached in. It was my leather case. My kit. Didn't remember bringing it.

I took it out, worked at the lock, and popped myself right in. I was amazed again at how simple it was. Pushed the door and let it swing open.

Nothing in there. Darkness and thunder. I stepped in, shut the door behind me. The air was thick, a dark solid of stale cigars and Scotch.

Waited for a minute, tried to let my eyes adjust, and began to see the dim outlines of crates and a forklift. Somewhere, far back, the presence of trucks. Felt like I was stepping into a tomb, the first to enter in years, the first to feel the mummy's curse.

Another flash, and the warehouse was lit instantly, strobe-like, through the large window above Russ's office. Outlines stayed burned on my eyes as I made my way along the wall of crates. I managed a ten-count, and the thunder hit. Moved my hand along rough wood, splinters digging in, and I felt the edge of the crates. There was an empty space beyond, a central area, where, in daylight, trucks pulled in and were unloaded.

Someone was out there.

A figure stood at the center of the loading bay. It stood, a deeper black against the darkness. I thought I recognized the shape. I saw him clearly in the next flash of lightning.

Eddie stood, head down. His shirt was caked with a Rorschach pattern of dried blood. He slid out of the darkness and raised his head, eyes glazed over, one of them staring off into black space. He smiled, toothy, purple-pink gums seeming to never end.

You fucked up, man, and when you fuck up, you never come back . . .

Eddie moved toward me, moved against the black current. He was in front of me before I could move. I felt his moist touch as he grabbed me by the shoulders. I was suddenly dark. Inside. Dark like the night.

Then he was gone.

I was in Russ's office. Cigars and Scotch stronger in here. I could see the safe, a thick black square, outlined against the wall.

They'd never expect you to do it, Eddie whispered in my head. *They'd never expect it . . .*

☆

I stepped out into the night, my jacket balled up and full of money. I cradled it in my hands, held it close to my body so none of the money would fall out. Looked back once at the warehouse, a dark, solid haunted house.

As I walked back toward the jetty I listened to the shifting gravel. Overhead, the clouds bloomed, pale bursts from within.

seven

I went straight to her place, stopping once to stuff the money into a plastic bag that was blowing around on the sidewalk. The dark windows of her building glowed purple, like bruised, beaten eyes.

The front door was too solid, had too many locks on it, and I couldn't pick my way in. I stepped off the curb, bent, and took some pebbles from the planters that lined the sidewalk. I threw a few at her window, backing out into the street as I did, trying to get a better shot. My first throw veered to the left and hit the neighbor's window with a sharp crack that seemed much louder than it should have. I waited for a light to come on, or for somebody to stick their head out, looking around for the ass-hole with the rocks, but nobody did. I threw another and this one hit Missy's window square in the middle. No light came on. Nothing. I threw another, and it hit just like the other one. Perfect center. Still nothing. Not a damned thing.

I crossed the street, sat on the steps of another building, and waited. Didn't know for what or for how long, but I did it anyway.

One of the skinny alley cats came out from behind a garbage can and approached the steps, head down, crouching almost, like it was stalking a mouse. I held my hand out, rubbed my fingers together.

"Come on, kid."

The cat stopped and raised its head a bit, black eyes getting wider. Then it approached and brushed against my hand.

"Hiya, beastie."

She was a little cat. I could feel every bone in her body. I pet her, and she purred. We sat together that way as the sun started taking a foothold in the sky.

A few lights started coming on in her building, and my heart began to beat a little faster. I couldn't stop thinking about what I'd say to her, and how she'd react when she saw the money. There were a million things I wanted to say. I couldn't think straight enough to remember them. I just knew I wanted to get the hell out of town and take her with me. Didn't know where we'd go. Didn't think it mattered.

Finally, some guy in a sweatsuit came jogging out of the building. Looked like he was a banker, or had some other occupation that caused premature baldness. Probably didn't know if he was running to or from the heart attack. I was off my feet, running for the door before the guy was even halfway down the steps. He didn't see me though. He had headphones on and was cruising down the street to his own beat. I stuck my arm between the door and the frame before it could shut and grabbed the handle with my other hand.

I took the steps two at a time, almost hopped up them like a kid on Christmas morning. I walked along the hall, trying to be quiet, my steps quick and purposeful.

I stood in front of her door for a moment, my hand held out, ready to knock. Tried to think of what to say and couldn't. Before I could stop myself I was knocking on her door. I listened for movement from the other side. Knocked again, my knuckles tapping the door. I set the money down between my feet. There was nothing from the other side, not a sound. I took out the kit. Her lock was old and easy. There was no deadbolt or chain on the door. A satisfying click, and the lock disengaged.

I pushed the door and let it swing open. The blinds on the other side of the hall were drawn, bluish morning light was spilling underneath them.

"*Missy?*"

My whisper traveled through the rooms, over the cold wood floors, along the bare walls. The place was empty.

I stepped in and walked through the hall, my footsteps the only sound. All the rooms were empty. Cleaned out. The living room, as sparse as it had been, now looked completely desolate. The Pan-Am poster of Rome was still there hanging by one corner, and the white tennis shoes were still out on the fire escape.

The kitchen was cleaned out. Two of the cabinets were half open. A box of baking soda had fallen and spilled on the floor. I could see her footprints in the white powder.

"Missy . . ."

I moved to her bedroom door. It was closed and I could see morning light coming from underneath. I pushed the door open and went in. Her bed was gone. The closets were open. Coat hangers lay scattered across the floor. Her window was open, and the curtains blew on the breeze. A stool sat in the middle of the room, a phone cord wrapped around one of its legs like a vine leading to nowhere. There was a small, light-blue box sitting on it. I walked over and picked it up. An envelope was tied to the box with a length of string. It said "B" on it. I opened it and read:

> I knew you'd find a way in. I left this present for you. It's too early to be getting Christmas gifts, but I always do my shopping early, so you'll just have to accept it. You were a nice guy and I liked you. I'm sorry.
>   M.

I opened the box. Saw something metallic, shining under cotton. It was a bullet. There was a small scrap of paper folded under it. Another note. Delicate handwriting.

> He was supposed to give this to you tomorrow night.

I went in the living room and dropped the money on the

floor. Leaned back against the wall and slid down. I sat on the hard floor, next to my bag of money, and stared at the crooked poster across the room.

I knew where she was. Felt it deep down in my stomach, a big black ball of centipedes squirming around in there.

eight

There were two hundred steps from the top of the hill to the docks. I held on to the rail, and took each one. Walked at my own pace. Somewhere out on the water, a buoy was sloshing around, its single green light blinking like the eyes of a tired cat. I could see the boats tied along the docks far beneath me.

My mind was white, clouded in haze. My mind was pure.

✧

The *Testament* was empty and dark. The colorful paper globes hung mute and dull from their line.

I climbed up onto the rear deck and tried the door. Locked. Went along the side deck. Didn't know if it was starboard or stem or stern. I tried some of the other doors. Same. All locked.

As I walked along the front, I looked across the bay to the city. She stood, shining on, thin streams of light, cars on the expressway, the only movement around her base. People going out to their lives. Some ending, some beginning. The clouds overhead were lit in false orange light, brimstone, the flames of Vesuvius raining down.

The first door I tried on the other side was unlocked. A dim light shone down on the hall. The black void of stairs lay at the other end. I shut the door behind me, moved through the hall, and tried each of the doors. I barely touched each of the knobs, hardly turned them at all. They were all locked. As I went along, I remembered what the rooms had looked like, small cabins, bed and bathroom in each. Then Leo's office, desk facing the door, and a small closet. Went to the stairs and walked down the first two. Didn't let myself go completely down into the darkness. I could make out the square of floor down there, could see a few tables and a couple of chairs. The disco ball reflected the hall light and sent squares of feeble amber through the black. Nobody down there.

I went back along the hall, back the way I had come, and climbed the stairs leading out to the decks. Came up into the room with the white shag carpet. The mirrored room with the glass tables and big TV. The room where I was tied and beaten. It was dark, but light came in from the harbor and shot through the empty spaces. I could see fine in here. It was as though a full moon were shining right down on me.

There was a note taped to the front of the TV. I peeled it off and read it: *don't touch VCR! taping Match Game!*

Videotapes lined the cabinet where the TV sat. They were lined up in rigid order, each one labeled. I pulled one out with a date on it. 10/27. Just a few days ago.

Sat down on the white carpet, set the money beside me, and turned the TV on. I hit the eject button and pulled out Leo's tape. Fuck him and his show. Popped 10/27 in the VCR, and hit play.

Shaky, hand held camera. It was shot on the *Testament*, in the same room where I was sitting. Everything was bright white, people dressed up and sitting around one of the low glass tables. The sound was distorted with laughter, and then the guy holding the camera, it must have been Leo, said, "*Let's see what you've got there ...*" The camera spun and there she was. Missy sat on the floor, two guys next to her. Behind her, on the couch, a girl let her arms drape over the side. Missy's eyes were narrow and glazed. Everybody was stoned. The camera tilted down to the tabletop and the screen went white in a pile of cocaine. "*Give me that or pour me another,*" someone said. The camera panned back over to Missy and slowly zoomed in on her. Her eyes filled the screen. "*Who loves you, baby?*" Leo asked. She looked ahead for a moment, then her gaze fixed on the lens. She stared right at me. "*You do.*"

The picture cut out, followed by static and another picture trying to come in. The tape skipped around a bit, and I hit the tracking button. The picture came back in, but it was dark. I could hear footsteps. Someone breathing. It seemed to be hand held again. I saw a street lamp and a stop sign. Then it was gone.

I sat on the floor, in the dark, my face practically buried in the screen. The glow of the TV bounced around the room. I sat on white shag and stared at the static on the screen. My mind swirled. Thoughts refused to gel.

＊

It took a minute or two, but I finally got it together. The haze faded.

I stumbled back down the hall. Made it to the door and the cool night air beyond.

＊

The city loomed in the background. I didn't look back.

I climbed the two hundred stairs, pausing once in the middle to sit on a bench. Thought I might have a heart attack. I listened to a buoy clang somewhere out on dark waters. Boats cruised silently below, lit up like flaming lily pads. Felt like I was getting a head rush, all the blood flowing through my head, colors rising and fading, clouding my sight. I brought a hand up and rubbed my eyes, tried to find some kind of stability, an anchor.

A wind rose up, rolled over the hill, and slithered down the stairs. The chill ran up my shirtsleeves, my skin erupting in gooseflesh. My eyes began to dry, my lips, too.

"*Hey.*"

The voice came from below. I turned, half expected to see her there, smiling and climbing the stairs toward me, white hands on railings. But there was no one, just stairs.

Then I climbed the rest of the way up, and had a drink from the water fountain at the top.

✳

The streets were a blur of light and sound. I heard nothing. I saw nothing.

I held the bag under one arm, half tucked under my coat.

Felt warmth on my face. Tears. Tears of anger.

nine

I made my way back home. Saw a few hurried, dusky shapes on the move, going up stairs, getting into cars. Everybody had their business, and they stuck to it.

I walked past the tobacco shop to my stairs. Cradled the money under my arm, and took a look back. Nobody on the street down here, only wet swirls in the lamp's glow. I went up. Stuck my key in the lock, and pushed the door open.

I stepped into my hallway and fumbled around for the light switch.

Raindrops began tapping the windows.

I turned and started into my room. I'd need a bag, a few clothes, toothbrush, and everything else that I couldn't think about. No focus. My thoughts were blasted in a million directions, threads running between them, web-like, a maze of confusion.

His shape was the first thing I really saw. Dark. He was standing by the window, an aura of street light surrounding him.

I stopped, held the money to my chest.

Vaughn stepped forward, his gun wavering. Where his eyes should've been, there were only wide black sockets. His boots squeaked on the linoleum. He stepped out of the dark and into the room's dim light, shadows leaving his eyes. They weren't empty sockets at all, just ringed. He hadn't slept in awhile. He glanced down at the bag, then back up to me.

"Just give me the money and get the hell out of here."

"No." I held the bag tighter.

Vaughn did a half-step, pulled the hammer back.

"I'm keeping it."

"They want you dead!"

"They'll be the dead ones." I started toward him.

Vaughn leveled on me, took aim.

I shut my eyes. Waited for the impact somewhere on my body.

When I opened my eyes, the hall was empty.

I went to the window and looked into the street. Thought I saw Vaughn running across the intersection further down. As he stepped up on the curb, he slipped in a puddle, almost lost it. Then he was gone, smothered in haze.

I never saw him again.

What a Difference a Day Makes

By ANNE BRICE
CONTRIBUTING EDITOR

... when, in fact, it has not only been the waterfront area businesses that have suffered over the last year. The entire city is feeling the crunch, perhaps even more than economically.

"People don't come out like they used to," said Rocky Trudeau, who owns a bar near Mason Park. "It used to be packed here on Fridays and weekends. Never had trouble making my bills. This place was always full of college kids. Now it's a ghost town around here. The kids don't laugh no more ..."

From the *East Bay Register*
(March 15, Opinion Section, pg. 3)

ten

Last car. Nobody around.

Lights flickered on both sides of the aisle. I walked, oblivious to everything around me, swaying with the car and the clackety-clack of the tracks, one hand up and sliding along the safety rail.

Made it to the door, dropped the bag down between my feet, and looked out through the window.

The city was falling away, shrinking against the dark blue night. Raindrops ran and smeared in map-like patterns across the window. The city looked like a crown, buildings lit and shining, a white glow filling the mist.

Then, a tunnel, and it was gone. Lost in pinpoint black. For some damned reason, I thought of Missy's plates, the ones she had brought out that rainy night not so long ago. The ones with the snake on them, biting its own tail. Picked up the bag and held it tight, up close against my chest. Never took my eyes off the window and the last trails of light.

I backed away, bumped into the last seats. Turned and sat, facing forward again.

The snake. Ruben would've started in about cycles and karma and time.

I sat and kept holding the bag on my lap. Had to loosen my grip a bit, though. One of my hands was shaking, a low tremble. I looked at it, let go of the bag, and raised my hand, turning it a little. I could almost hear it, low and humming, like dragonfly wings.

Cycles.

My eyes blurred, teared up, and I rubbed them.

I sat in the swaying dark and thought only of time and that no matter where I ran to, nothing would ever change. The more things seemed to change, the more they stayed the same.

Folded my arms across the bag and squeezed it tight. If all beautiful women are murderers, I thought, then Time is the most beautiful woman of all.

Graffiti on the corner of DiLeo & 45th:

Better Red than dead

I'd like to thank the following:

John and Anne Lester for love and support above and beyond the call of duty, Rich Linder, Martin Nakell, Mark Axelrod, and Gabrielle Middaugh.

I'd also like to thank Jodi-Renée Kaplan for helping me get this book ready to show publishers. Your love and support constantly amazes me. I couldn't have done it without you. Aspiring writers drop everything and go to www.thescribe.web.com.

Last but not least, a thousand thanks to Tom Fassbender and Jim Pascoe. It's been a pure pleasure working with you guys. Thanks for helping me make this a better book.